Forward

After working on this book for over three years, I am glad to be able to offer it to you. We have had some technical delays as well as taking time out to adjust to schooling choices for each child, but now the book is finished. I hope you will be encouraged to not give up on your dreams and be willing to live "outside the box."

There are those that I would like to thank for helping me with this book. To my husband David I appreciate your continual encouragement to me to see this book to fruition. To our four children Craig, Scott, Bonny Jean and Suzannah, thank you for providing so much joy in my life and so much material for this book. Craig, thank you for asking the question "Mom, Why Can't We Just Be A Normal Family?" You asked this when you found out we were really going on this trip, and you were going to be leaving friends, school, and sports for a whole year!

My thanks to Robert J. Tamasy for being the project editor and Beth Close for putting the pages into book form. Thank you to Reuel Cornelison for the cover illustration and to Sarah Miller for editing the book. I appreciate my college friend, Betty Sheryl Cook and also Farrar Moore for helping proof. To all of my family and friends who read my trip E-Mails and encouraged me to write this book, I thank you.

To you, the reader, thank you for sharing in our adventure. We realize a twelve-month. fifty-state tour may be outside the realm of possibility for most families, but all should consider ways of stepping outside the norm, looking for something that will prove to be both unusual and life-changing. As we chose to "not do the normal," may you in your own life be encouraged to live the life, God has given you to the fullest.

Contents

"Mom, Why Can't We Just Be A Normal Family?"

Sally Thomas Worland is available for speaking engagements.

You may contact her at the following address:

385 Hidden Hollow Lane

Chickamauga, Georgia 30707

E-mail *sallyworland@mindspring.com*

Also for additional copies of

"Mom, Why Can't We Just Be A Normal Family?"

You may order from the same address.

Robert J. Tamasy, Project Editor

Publishing Company, CampCrest Publishing

ISBN#0-9763257-0-5

CHAPTER ONE

U.S.A., Here We Come!

As our family started out on that evening in mid-April of 2001, on the final leg of our nearly twelve-month tour of the United States, the travel assignment seemed simple enough: To leave Worland, Wyoming, in our thirty-one-foot Coachman Leprechaun recreational vehicle and drive across the Big Horn Mountains en route to Buffalo, Wyoming. It was bitterly cold, but we didn't anticipate any problems. Traveling at night would help my husband, David, keep on schedule for his next meeting several days later in St. Louis, Missouri.

He was at the wheel and I sat across from him in the passenger's seat as we drove up and down and around the mountains, something we had done frequently during our travels over the past several months. Several days earlier, we had driven from Yellowstone National Park through the Rocky Mountains to Worland, so we expected an uneventful journey to our next destination in the scenic Northwest.

If we had been traveling by day, the view would have been spectacular as we followed the Big Horn Mountain Pass eastward. However, all we could see was the road ahead, illuminated by the RV's headlights. When snowflakes began to fall in front of us, David and I felt a little concern, but snow we had encountered at other points on our trip had not presented much of a problem, so our anxiety level was fairly low. Our emotions escalated as the snow became heavier and the wind began blowing extremely hard. Behind us in the RV, our four children — Craig, Scott, Bonny Jean, and Suzannah — were busy playing games and watching videos, about ready to go to bed, not yet sensing any of our tension about the impending weather.

Suddenly, we found ourselves caught up in a blizzard, with snow and ice showering the RV and reducing our visibility to a matter of a few feet. When the storm's low clouds settled on top of the mountain we were on, it became even more difficult to see the roadway. For all we knew, ours was the only vehicle on the mountain pass that night. There were no cars ahead of us or behind us, and it had been a long time since a car had passed going the other direction.

The snow, ice, and fog were not our only reasons for concern. We could not see how close we were to the edge of the narrow, winding mountain road. The drop-off was steep, and in many places there were no guardrails to offer protection or warn us of a sudden drop. Despite the frigid air, I rolled down my window to hold out a flashlight and try to see where the edge was. Since the road was becoming increasingly slippery, sliding off the side was as great a worry for us as accidentally steering into danger. We had no idea how far the drop was and certainly didn't want to find out.

I could almost imagine the headlines: "Family of Six Takes Icy Plunge Off Mountainside." That was not exactly how I envisioned the final account of our ambitious coast-to-coast, fifty-state adventure.

We were growing frantic, wondering how we were going to get through this dilemma. I have heard some people say, "When all else fails, pray," but over the years my family has grown accustomed to hearing me declare — whether prompted by a glorious sunset or an impending crisis — "I feel a prayer coming on." At that moment, we *all* felt a prayer coming on! Throughout our cross-country journey, we had found prayer to be a delightful and faithful companion, but this night we were depending on it more than ever.

Suddenly, hope appeared! Directly on the next hill in front of us, we saw the yellow lights of a snowplow clearing a path for us down the mountain. We didn't know where it had come from; it seemed almost as if it had just dropped from the sky. One moment we could see nothing ahead of us, and the next moment there were the comforting lights from the snowplow, pointing the way as it pushed aside the snow and ice, leading us to safety. As David commented later, sometimes angels come in the form of snowplows!

I think the driver of the snowplow must have noticed that we were following him, but he never acknowledged it, even after we got to the bottom of the mountain and stopped to thank him. (Have you ever wanted to hug a snowplow?) Apparently, he felt he was just doing his job and did not realize how imperiled we had felt on the icy mountain roadway. I don't know if he had ever experienced a miracle in his own life, but to us, this stocky man with a thick mustache, wearing layers of warm clothing and a woolen hat with covers for his ears — whose name we will never know — *was* a miracle to us.

Later we learned the mountain road had been officially closed as the weather began to deteriorate. By that time we had already been driving on the pass for quite a while, and there was no way for us to have known about the travelers' warning.

Safely down the mountain, the weather improved enough for us to drive on to Buffalo. Along the way, we praised God and thanked Him for answering our prayers in such a wonderful and unexpected manner. In Buffalo we found a modest little hotel where we could spend the night. Even the fact that the hotel's water heater was broken (along with several other minor problems) did not diminish our joy in having been delivered from danger by the timely appearance of a snowplow that just "happened" to be there when we needed it.

The Bible says that we often don't know how to pray as we should, and this certainly was a good example. While we were praying anxiously during the ice storm, I don't think it occurred to any of us to ask, "God, please send a snowplow," but that's exactly what He did. For those who live in the Southeastern United States, as we do, the appearance of a snowplow is an infrequent occurrence. Entire winters may go by without our sighting one, or feeling the need for one. But if you ask any member of the Worland family, we will now assure you that the snowplow is one of mankind's greatest inventions.

This was one of the most traumatic — and dramatic — experiences during our travels, but it is just one example of countless times that we witnessed the Lord providing for our needs. Whether it was staying just a day or two ahead of other snowstorms, finding someone to assist when we had mechanical problems, or locating a suitable place to spend the night, God was unbelievably creative in handling situations of varying complexities that arose as our eager family of six wheeled across the United States.

How About a Little Trip — to Fifty States?

But how does a family with four children, who ranged from seven to twelve years old when we started, embark on a journey such as ours — a journey that spanned an entire year and more than 43,000 roadway miles (via recreational vehicle and rental cars), plus an additional 20,000 miles we spent in the air flying to the only two states (Alaska and Hawaii) that were beyond the reach of our RV?

To tell the truth, our trip was more than twenty years in the making. Early in my life I had the opportunity to do a lot of travel, going to Hawaii with my family; and then as a single adult, traveling to Alaska with a friend; taking part in a cattle drive in Montana; traveling on a wagon train in Wyoming; snow skiing in Colorado; and a lot of other great experiences. I had been to forty-nine states before I got married and finally got to the last state on my list (Wisconsin) after David and I had married. I always thought it was great to have accomplished that goal.

It was awe-inspiring to see firsthand the beauty and diversity of our great nation — its geography, people, and culture — from region to region. Even prior to meeting David, I had envisioned getting married and having our family enjoy the same experience of traveling to each of the fifty states. I had been fortunate enough also to travel to some other countries, and that was fun, but for some reason none of them held the mystique for me of seeing and enjoying different parts of the United States.

I was so convinced that one day I would have a family that would travel together from coast to coast, I even started saving frequent flyer air miles from my trips while still a single person. Soon after David and I married in 1984, we discussed this goal and began planning and praying to that end. We had no idea when or how the trip would come about, but we sensed that this was something God would make possible in His own time, so we left it at that.

In the early 1990s, on several occasions we tried to calculate what it would cost us to take our family, after our first three children had been born, on a fifty-state tour of our nation. Every time our conclusion was the same: Too much! There was not only the financial cost, but also the expenditure of the time it would take to crisscross the United States until every state had been traveled.

We live in a rustic, country setting in the northwest Georgia mountains, about seventeen miles from Chattanooga, Tennessee; we knew that if we sold our house we could probably finance the trip, but that was never a serious consideration. My parents, Bonny Jean and Tommy Thomas, own 140 acres surrounding our property, and to sacrifice not only our home, but also access to the lake, creeks, view of nearby mountains, and the pastures where our horses, dogs, and cats roam would have been too great a cost. The short-term gain of seeing the U.S.A., in our estimation, was not worth the long-term loss of parting with such an ideal setting for raising our children.

So we clung to our dream of traveling across our entire nation but concluded that if God had indeed planted that desire in our hearts, He would have to provide the answer to our question of how?

We weren't completely passive, sitting on the proverbial stump waiting for a Divine solution. We shared our desire with our children. and they became excited about the trip. We all talked and prayed about the possibility of making a fifty-state journey one day, and our children prompted us to start saving coins in a can on which they had written, "Year 2000 Trip."

One day the Lord did answer our prayers. He did it, however, in a way we could never have anticipated.

David had been the Director of the Chattanooga Christian Community Foundation in Chattanooga, Tennessee, for seven years, and in August of 1999, he was invited to join the staff of the National Christian Foundation (NCF) based in Atlanta, Georgia. Several prominent leaders had started the Foundation in 1982 to provide assistance to individuals and groups wanting to maximize the effectiveness and use of financial resources entrusted to their care.

David became excited about the opportunity for two reasons. This would enable him to apply his skills and experience on a national basis, and we would not have to move our family from our beautiful rural surroundings. This would mean he would have to drive back and forth to Atlanta frequently, but we felt that was a fair trade-off.

Shortly before he officially assumed his new position with the National Christian Foundation, David was participating in a strategic planning session in Atlanta with some of the organization's leaders. One of the men in the meeting casually commented, "We sure wish we had a person in the office that would be willing to take an RV, travel with their family for about a year all around America, and tell people about our Foundation."

When he heard those words, David's jaw dropped. Almost in disbelief, he asked, "What did you say?" When the comment was repeated, that they wanted someone to travel across the country on behalf of the Foundation, David couldn't help but smile. "Well, you're looking at him."

His new employers all started to laugh. "Yeah, we're looking at you," one of them replied, "but what would your wife say about something like this?"

David simply shrugged his shoulders and responded, "Sally's bags were packed yesterday." Then he proceeded to explain our dream of taking our family around the United States, and how we had been praying about this for years. I think he told them an abbreviated version of our story, because he kept thinking, *This can't really be true,* but this initiated a discussion that several months later led to the Foundation's commitment to purchase an RV for our family's use.

If I had been the one in that meeting, I would have called David immediately. I might even have scheduled a press conference, or at least climbed to a nearby housetop so I could shout the good news. But David did none of the above. He simply drove home and waited to tell me face to face.

When he came in the door, I was in the kitchen cooking dinner. I could tell he was excited about something, but trying to keep it contained. Instead of blurting out what had happened, he greeted the children and me, and then we spent some time talking about the pleasantries of the day. But I kept wondering.

Finally, David looked at me and asked, "You know what they said to me at work today?" He proceeded to relate the conversation about someone dedicating about a year to tour the country and tell individuals and groups of local leaders about the National Christian Foundation and its services.

I reacted the only way I knew how. I said, "Thank you, God!" I felt He had answered our prayers and the desire of our hearts that we have had for all these years!

David cautioned, "Don't get your hopes all up. We don't know that this is going to happen." But I never had a moment of doubt. *Yes, it's going to happen,* I thought. *This is the way God wants it to happen.*

I can't remember exactly when we told our children — Craig, 12; Scott, 11; Bonny Jean, 9; and Suzannah, 7 — whether it was that evening or if we waited until we had a more concrete plan of action, but they were very excited. We began looking at maps of the United States and talking about some of the places we would be seeing. None of our children had been out West or to the northern states, so we told them they were in for some very special experiences.

Before long, however, we realized it is one thing to imagine taking such an ambitious journey — and quite another to actually begin planning for it. There was a lot of hard work yet to be done before David, the children, and I could announce, "California (or wherever), here we come!" My dreams of taking this trip, which I had nurtured fondly since my early adult years, were still months from becoming a reality.

Getting the Picture

As you might expect, we took many photos throughout our trip. (We are sprinkling some of these throughout this book, just to give you a visual idea of what we saw and did.) Partly out of necessity, we discovered the wonders of the digital camera since it could get extremely expensive buying new rolls of film to capture every stage of our trip. With a digital camera, however, we could be more selective since after we took a photo, we could review it and determine whether we wanted to keep it, erase it from the camera disk, or simply redo the shot.

However, I also realized that with a digital camera, the old saying, "Pictures don't lie" is false in itself. In fact, I have concluded that digital photos should be labeled either "fiction" or "non-fiction." David, who was our primary photographer, not only enjoyed capturing images to represent our travels, but also took great pleasure in seeing how he could digitally manipulate the photos on the computer.

For instance, through the wonders of technology he could make a mountain appear much larger in a photo. He could insert a rainbow wherever he wanted it, he could sharpen the photo, or modify it in many other ways, depending on his whim at that moment.

Personally, I felt that somehow it just wasn't right to distort the images the camera had captured, but David assured me that I merely had an "antiquated opinion" that needed enlightenment in view of modern technology. Finally, I decided that I had better watch my words, or David might just replace me in the photos with Julia Roberts! By the way, the pictures in this book are the real thing.

Of course, the greatest "pictures" of our trip are the memories that have been etched indelibly in our minds, recollections of fond experiences that I'm sure will be recalled many times in the years to come.

I HAVE INCLUDED THE E-MAILS THAT I SENT TO FAMILY AND FRIENDS FROM OUR TRIP. THEY ARE IN THE ORDER THEY WERE WRITTEN EVEN THOUGH THE BOOK IS NOT IN CHRONOLOGICAL ORDER. SOME OF THE E-MAILS ARE REPETITIVE OF THINGS WRITTEN IN THE BOOK SO YOU MAY CHOOSE TO READ THE E-MAILS ALL AT ONCE. PLACED THROUGHOUT THE BOOK ARE VARIOUS PICTURES FROM OUR TRAVELS.

(left to right)
Craig, David, Bonny Jean, Scott, Suzannah, Sally and Smokey

Our Home at Hidden Hollow in Chickamauga, Georgia

Hidden Hollow lake

U. S. A., Here We Come!

I could almost imagine the headlines:

2 Sections

NORTHERN WYOMING

Daily News

SERVING THE BIG HORN BASIN

95th Year, No. 75 | Saturday, April 14, 2001 | 50 Cents

The Worland, Wyoming newspaper did an article on our trip.

Worland, Wyoming, our kind of town!

>>> "Dave Worland" <daveworland@mindspring.com>
08/26/00 9:02 PM >>>
8/26/00

Dear Family and Friends,

Well Hello from Philadelphia. We have put over 5000 miles on the RV and are learning what close quarters means! Tomorrow, we tour Philly which is history in the making. We toured Gettysburg the last couple of days and were amazed at the feelings within us as we reflected on the Civil War. Later this week, we will be in Washington DC and then Williamsburg where we participate in a week for home-schoolers, then on to New York City, Boston, and New England. Of course, there are a lot of side trips as well. What wonderful history we are all learning.

Dave is working hard for his job with NCCF and has had a lot of meetings as well as working on his office items. We are the most technologically advanced RV going down the road as he works on his cell phone, computer and runs the printer while I drive. When he drives, I am enjoying the beautiful scenery although I still feel we live in one of the most beautiful areas in the nation.

We have enjoyed visiting some different churches We have met some really nice folks.

Please know we are thinking about you all. If you know of anyone that would like to be included in on our E-Mails please have them contact us.

Take care and God Bless each of you.

Love.

Sally, David, Craig, Scott, Bonny Jean and Suzannah Worland

P.S. One of the first things the boys look for at the campground is a basketball goal. They even played with a basketball player who played for Syracuse. I've told them that I may have to get a peach basket for them to hang on the RV. After all that is how I started playing basketball.

>>> "Dave Worland" <daveworland@mindspring.com>
09/6/00>>>
9/6/00

September 6, 2000

Dear Family and Friends,

Hello from Williamsburg, Va. We are staying in the historic area and have had a wonderful time reliving life in the colonial days. We were in Washington, DC last week where we did about everything we could possibly do. We even went to church on Sunday morning at New York Avenue Presbyterian Church and sat in the pew that Abraham Lincoln "rented." It is also the church where Peter Marshall was the minister. We also went to Arlington Cemetery, Supreme Court Bldg. (where they supposedly have a basketball court on the top), The Capitol, in the White House, the Smithsonian, "The Call for Christian families on the mall," Washington Memorial, Lincoln Memorial, Vietnam Memorial, Ford's Theatre, Washington Hotel at night for dinner and the daytime for lunch (the view was beautiful) , and the naval museum. As you can see it was really neat.

We appreciate so many of you responding to our E-Mails. It is fun to keep up with things at home. The boys wanted me to ask Coach K if they had some new students come to CCS that are good basketball players?

David has really been getting a lot done with his work and has also had a lot of good meetings. The homeschooling is progressing and I am filled with questions for those of you better equipped at it than I am! What a fun (most of the time) challenge.

Take care and let us hear from you.

Cordially,
Sally, David, Craig, Scott, Bonny Jean, and Suzannah

CHAPTER TWO

Wagons Ho
Getting Ready to Leave

Planning to spend about twelve months traveling around the U.S.A. with two adults and four children obviously would require a lot more preparation than a weekend trip to the beach or a week on a lake. We couldn't just tell everyone to pack a suitcase and line up on the porch for departure. Although we had dreamed about an opportunity like this for years, we were amazed at how many details — large and small — we had to work through.

For instance, we needed to determine what would be our means of transportation. We had to make sure our home would still be intact when we returned. The kids had the small matter of finishing their school year. And I had a commitment to fulfill — the annual summer camps that I had conducted for more than twenty-five years; before we took to the highways for our big adventure. About 160 children and 40 staff were expecting to spend time with us at Camp Hidden Hollow during the two one-week sessions.

The children completed their classes at school successfully without letting the trip distract them too much, so one prerequisite was out of the way. Next came the two consecutive one-week camps. Getting ready for the camp sessions in June of 2000, along with looking ahead to our trip, presented a real challenge but with the Lord's help we made it.

Next came the question of our "wheels." The National Christian Foundation agreed to purchase the RV that would be best suited for our needs, with the understanding that it would be sold and the Foundation would recoup the proceeds once our travels were over.

We settled on a thirty-one-foot Coachman Leprechaun. Our requirements had been first, that it comfortably accommodate all six of us, because we were going to be spending many, many hours in it; and second, that it be affordable. The idea was not to purchase the Ritz on wheels, just something that would provide reasonable living space and be equipped with the amenities we would need. Since the Foundation would not be keeping it permanently, we also needed to select a model that could easily be resold.

The Leprechaun seemed to fit the bill. It had a slide-out side to make the living room area larger by eighteen inches, and appliances in the modest kitchen included a small refrigerator, a microwave, a compact but serviceable stove, and an oven. However, we already knew that we would be using a specially-fitted propane stove on the outside of the RV for most our cooking, since we preferred not to prepare many meals indoors because of lingering food odors.

The RV would provide ample sleeping accommodations: An overhang above the cab had a bed, which is where David and I would sleep; the couch in the living room could be converted into a small bed; a table also could be made into a bed; and in the back, we had two sets of bunk beds, even with seat belts, installed. In all, we could utilize as many as eight beds at one time, so it was never necessary for the children to share beds. Knowing that when we stayed in hotels they would often have to share beds to save on expenses, we wanted to be sure each child had a place they could call their own while we were on the road.

One of the bunk beds had to be located in front of the RV's emergency exit, so that bed had to be constructed shorter than the others in order for the exit door to open if needed. This ended up being where Bonny Jean slept, but she was short enough that the reduced length of the bed wasn't a problem for her.

Each child had an individual cubbyhole that David had constructed where they could store their clothes and other belongings. We definitely would be living in limited space, but it was interesting to see how much the kids managed to pack into their respective areas. As you can imagine with four children, it would have been very easy to have all their stuff scattered throughout the RV, so the storage spaces David built helped us keep things where we could readily find them. He also built a drawer under the couch where I would store all of our homeschooling materials. It may sound confining, but it actually worked out very well.

David was wonderful with all the work he did preparing the RV for our trip. He even devised a laundry chute that would go to a compartment at the bottom of the motor home to collect our dirty clothing, installed a connection for a small TV in the room at the rear, and hooked up a camera and monitor next to the driver's seat so we could see what was behind us whenever we needed to back up.

Also in the cab of the RV were a computer that told us the altitude and outside temperature, a compass for navigation, and a mechanism to adjust the fuel mix in the generator we used for appliances in the RV when the altitude changed significantly. It was hardly the most elaborate vehicle we could have found, but we had to admit it turned fairly high-tech.

Even though a thirty-one-foot RV sounds fairly large, space was still at a premium, so we determined to put limits on everything we took with us. We restricted everyone to seven changes of clothes, meaning we all would have to wear the items once a week. The bad news was that after a while, we certainly would grow tired of wearing the same things over and over. The good news was that except for each other, no one we met along the way would know the difference. Even though we had to wear the same outfits for church each Sunday, for example, since we would be attending a different church each week, there would be no one to wonder why we always looked the same.

The food supply was a real challenge. Since our home is out in the country, miles from the nearest grocery store or mall, I had become very accustomed to shopping in bulk for long periods of time. When I went to buy food for the trip the first time, I overbought quite a bit. David saw me laboring with the carts and he began laughing and said, "You forgot we aren't home." As is often the case, you learn through trial and error. It wouldn't take long before I realized that all I could buy at one time was food for about two or three meals.

As we took the RV out for a few test rides, the children quickly decided that was the perfect way to travel. It was a huge difference from riding in a van, as they were accustomed to doing. They had plenty of room to move around in the RV and their excitement began to build as they thought about touring America's highways in such an expansive vehicle.

Details, Details, and More Details

As the time to start our trip approached, it was amazing all the little details we uncovered. For instance, we had to make arrangements for our mail through a commercial mail service. Periodically, we would arrange for them to forward our mail to a designated location so that when we arrived in that city, our mail would be waiting for us. (More on this in chapter 4.)

To reduce the volume of mail that would have to be forwarded, we put as many of our bills as we could on automatic draft from our bank, including our house payment, our utilities, and the cell phone. As we traveled, some of the bills we did receive could be paid through our bank by computer. Generally, this would work out well, although we did encounter problems with paying an additional sum each month against the principal of our mortgage. As I write this, more than a year later, we still haven't fully resolved what has and has not been paid on our mortgage.

We turned off our water, since we would not be needing it while we were gone, and set the thermostat just high enough to prevent the pipes from freezing during the winter months. My parents agreed to come up to our house once a week and make sure everything seemed all right while we were away.

We took our four horses to Signal Mountain — about twenty-five miles away — and put them in a pasture that I use for Recreation Ranch, a therapeutic horsemanship center for the disabled. We arranged for a caretaker to feed and care for them. Periodically, I would call him to see if the horses were doing all right.

A Sampling of "Buyer's Remorse?"

One day, after we were well into our preparations for the trip, I walked out onto the front porch of the house. The view was breathtaking, with Lookout Mountain looming nearby and our lake reflecting the trees around it. *What other wonderful scenes from God's creation would we be experiencing over the upcoming months?* I wondered to myself.

Our oldest son, Craig, then 12, was on the swing nearby. Even though he had been in favor of the trip from the start, the reality of being away from home for seventh grade was starting to sink in. He was particularly concerned about missing out on playing for the seventh-grade basketball team, because he loves the sport so dearly, and also knew he would miss his friends. Even though Craig's temperament is typically upbeat, he understandably was having second thoughts, almost like the so-called buyer's remorse when one makes a major purchase and then begins reconsidering it. The adventure he had felt so excited about years earlier when we first started talking about it suddenly didn't seem like such a great idea.

As I walked toward the swing, I began telling him in some detail about how we would be traveling and explaining that "home" over most of the next twelve months would be very different from what we had grown accustomed to as a family.

Suddenly, Craig looked me directly in the eye and said, *"Mom, why can't we just be a normal family?"* This opened the door to a really good discussion. I told him that I could understand his misgivings but tried to console him by pointing out the benefits we would derive from the trip. Along with the travel experiences, I reminded him that it would give us all a unique opportunity to bond as a family.

To that he replied, "Mom, we live out here in the middle of the sticks with no one else around. Who else do we have to bond with here?" Yes, I agreed that our home environment already had enabled us to bond, but I assured him that the trip would bond us even more closely together.

A True Working "Vacation"

One of the things we needed to keep foremost in our minds in preparing for our trans-U.S.A. journey was that this was not an extended family vacation. Our trip was being made possible by David's job with the Foundation, and every effort had to be made in setting up our new recreational vehicle to facilitate his work throughout our travels.

David had been involved in charitable foundation work for nine years, mostly interacting with the local Christian community and church foundations. His duties on our trip would be primarily to respond to organizations like these in more than forty cities — some just getting started and others that were already established — to help their boards, steering committees, and individual leaders determine what their objectives were and how aligning with the National Christian Foundation could be to their benefit.

The plan was to work principally with high-income, high-net-worth individuals to show them how they, as a network of donors, could have a strong impact on their communities, ultimately to advance the cause of Jesus Christ.

David would offer to them a whole series of tools and techniques that NCF had developed since its founding in 1982, including how to provide philanthropic counseling to donors and other creative means for showing them how to become faithful stewards of the financial resources God had entrusted to them. While our family was excited about the trip in general, the children and I all had a sense of how important these meetings could be toward transforming thousands of lives in these communities across the United States.

Because the trip would be so work-intensive for David, the vehicle not only had to accommodate our very active family of six, but also a computer, a combination printer, copier, and fax machine, two cell phones (one as a backup and also to ensure the maximum coverage area for calling in and out), a headset so he could talk on the phones and keep his hands free for other things, and all the wires needed to make all of our technological gadgets work properly.

Our RV certainly had to be one of the most technologically advanced of all the vehicles we passed throughout our travels. The devices didn't get us to our destinations any faster, but we were hardly ever out of communication range in one form or another. When I drove, David would be the "techie," fully connected to the Foundation and anyone else he needed to contact. When he took his turn driving, however, I would just sit back and enjoy the beautiful natural panorama of America (even though my personal bias is that our area in northern Georgia is one of the most gorgeous parts of the nation).

To receive faxes, David initially tried to have them sent directly through his computer, but for some reason that did not work as well as expected. So we depended on linking up to phone jacks whenever we stopped somewhere, whether that was at a motel, a client's office, or even at many of the camping grounds we visited. We were pleased to find out that many campgrounds have kept pace with the technological boom and even offer business centers for the convenience of their guests who, like us, were combining business with pleasure.

We understood that David's unusual working arrangement would require adjustments for all of us. David is extremely diligent at his job, and I knew there would be times when I would have to remind myself that it was his job that made it possible for us to take this adventure. Nevertheless, there were times when it seemed as if the phones were glued to his ears, since he stayed in frequent contact with the home office, people he would be getting together with in the days ahead, and other individuals that he needed to talk with to coordinate future meetings. David — and the rest of us — learned that having five people around you when you're trying to work is not an easy matter.

Because he was so busy preparing for meetings and getting his schedule lined up weeks and even months in advance, he wasn't able to reap as much enjoyment from the first part of the trip as he had expected, but after the initial time of adjustment, he was able to settle into a semblance of a routine and enjoy our travels much more.

There were times when the family and I had to go away from the RV, riding our bikes or doing some other type of activity, so David could get some peace and quiet. Eventually he would get up early in the morning, whether we were camping or in a hotel, to find a place by himself where he could work in solitude. He often would work for hours nonstop, and then would return and be able to spend some time with us.

When we arrived at cities where David had meetings, sometimes he would rent a car or the people with whom he was meeting would pick him up, take him to their meetings, and then bring him back to our RV home.

Plotting Our Path

As we started to envision our trip, we took out a large map of the United States and plotted out where David would have all of his meetings, city by city. Then we began to figure out a way we could very logically get to each state in conjunction with those meetings. For those states where he would not have any meetings, we built in flexibility so we could still spend some time there, at least to say we had been to each one and seen some of its unique features. As it turned out, there would be very few states that we would have to drive into, just to say we had gone there.

Since we would be covering such a vast geographic area, having a wide selection of maps readily available was a necessity. To enable us to systematically chart our progress along the trip, we purchased a magnetic, fifty-state map that we posted on the side of the RV so we could display each of the states we had visited, along with items that would represent activities we had experienced along the way.

Our first actual trip was to Florida in February of 2000 to attend the Journey family reunion (my maternal grandmother's side of the family), traveling through parts of Georgia and Alabama along the way. Then we went to St. Louis, Missouri, in June of 2000, where we took part in a Worland family reunion. We used that opportunity to rent an RV — literally taking a "test drive" — and visit several other northern states at the same time, including Indiana and New

York, as well as Ottawa, Ontario, Canada. These states we later revisited once our official U.S.A. tour got underway.

Stage one of our trip was to drive through Virginia and Maryland, stopping in Washington, D.C., then proceeding through Philadelphia, New York City, and Boston, as we worked our way through the New England states. At that time of the year, the weather was very pleasant and the scenery was delightful. (I'll elaborate about that portion of our trip in the next chapter.) This first stage would conclude at the end of October with a brief stop to visit some friends in Highlands, North Carolina; and then we would head home to enjoy the Thanksgiving and Christmas holidays in our real home.

We wanted to schedule this break for the family, but also it made sense from David's work perspective because meetings were difficult to schedule around the end of the year. This would give him a chance to catch his breath, get caught up with paperwork, and assess the effectiveness of his first meetings so he could make any needed adjustments for sessions he would be conducting in the upcoming months.

Stage two, we had determined, would start January 9, 2001, as we headed west, taking a northerly route through states like Wisconsin, Minnesota, Nebraska, North Dakota, and South Dakota. Because of the distance, we would be away from our real home for a much longer span of time. It would be in the winter, of course, and from a traveling standpoint it had seemed like it would be more practical to go south first, driving in the warmer climates. Because of how David's meetings were scheduled, however, we needed to go northward to the upper Midwest, with Brookings, South Dakota, being one of our initial destinations.

Where Do We Put The Bikes?

Before we embarked, one of the big debates had been whether we should take a car with us, pulling it behind the RV. We decided not to do that, and renting cars — coupled with the graciousness of people David met with who would provide transportation for him — worked out very well. As it turned out, the space behind the RV was needed for other purposes.

One of our greatest challenges was to determine how we could bring along some recreational equipment, such as our bicycles and basketballs. Even though we would be on the road, we are a very active family and equipment; such as bikes and basketballs, are necessities, not optional items. Initially, we thought we could manage with a specially made bike rack for the RV in which we could mount all six bicycles. However, the first time we tried it, it broke even before we had gotten out of our driveway. Actually, we had intended to get started on our trip and were going to stop first to visit briefly with some family members. A TV station had even sent a reporter and camera crew to do a brief feature on us as we set out on our journey. Because of the broken bike rack we had to delay our departure until the next morning. David removed the rack and tried to rebuild it. We were hopeful, but once again it never made it out of our driveway without pulling apart.

At that point we were starting to think we might need to find an affordable trailer to haul the bikes behind the RV, but we knew a trailer would make it more difficult to back up and maneuver the RV. Since we had a Christian Business Men's Committee family conference to attend near Asheville, North Carolina, before we officially set out on our journey, we held out hope that we could find someone in that area to repair and fortify our bike rack. Before leaving for North Carolina, we temporarily attached a rack for one of the bicycles onto the back of the RV and stuffed the other five bikes inside, knowing they would have to take up much-valued living space only for about four or five hours until we arrived at the conference site.

Obviously, our trip didn't get off to a great start. Some people even suggested, "Don't you think you're being told you shouldn't go?" But, we weren't discouraged in the least. We knew that just because God gives you something that you clearly believe you are supposed to do, that doesn't mean everything will go smoothly or be easy.

Between sessions at the conference in North Carolina we tried to find someone who could weld the bicycle rack properly so it wouldn't break again. We did find a man who tried, but once again, it broke as we were departing at the conclusion of the conference. Thankfully, none of our "breakdowns" occurred once our trip got underway. God was watching out for us even before our travels really began.

We concluded it would be best to forget about the bike rack idea and began looking for a trailer that could accommodate six bicycles, basketballs, and other equipment. We selected a trailer that we thought would work and headed back to the conference center to pick up our bicycles, but only four or five of the bikes would fit. We needed a larger trailer, so we went back to the trailer place to swap our trailer for one with more room. We found one that we felt certain would serve our purposes and bought it on the spot. A couple of hours later, with six bicycles and assorted recreational equipment jammed securely into the trailer, we headed off for the Northeastern United States.

Even with the earlier trial runs, we all had felt that our journey wouldn't officially get launched until after we had attended the five-day family conference and waved farewell to Lake Junaluska near Asheville, North Carolina. At last, after years of praying and months of planning, we were on our way!

So we turned north and hoped for the best — determined to monitor the Weather Channel every day. We simply trusted that God would direct our paths, as Solomon says in Proverbs 3:5-6, and would lead us away from or through any difficulties. Aside from our weather concerns, this travel sequence made the most sense, and we knew God's grace would enable us to navigate any adverse winter weather successfully.

Thankfully — and we attribute this to God's providential hand — weather never presented much of a problem for us. We did watch the weather map regularly so we could be aware if any severe storms were ahead of us, but for the most part, it seemed as if the Lord enabled us to remain just ahead of the snowstorms.

We found it humorous to read newspapers and watch weather reports, hearing about major snowstorms that would hit an area a day or two after we had passed through it. Most of the places we drove through in the north had snow on the ground, but it never got to a point where is seemed dangerous for us to proceed. There were a couple of times that we had to exert special caution while we were driving, but most of the time, we just sailed through the northern states even though the temperatures were blistering cold, often below zero.

Most of the southwestern states were reserved for the final leg of our trip and provided many of our highlights, including visits to ancient Indian dwellings, the Grand Canyon, the Petrified Forest, and the Painted Desert. We spent three full days in Texas alone, and we were able to see many parts of that huge and delightfully diverse state. Our concluding itinerary would take us west, eventually to the state of Washington, parking our RV for a seven-day vacation to Alaska, then continuing south through Oregon and California, and then east.

We would arrive back home in early-to mid-April, settle in for a few weeks, and then prepare to leave for the final stopping point of our tour of the U.S.A. — Hawaii. David did not have any meetings there, or in Alaska, but the frequent flyer miles we had accumulated over the years would prove handy in enabling all of us to fulfill our dream by visiting the fiftieth state, which was also fiftieth and last on our grand tour.

During the planning stage of our trip, we had decided it would be appropriate to select a theme verse from the Bible. We agreed that it should be, "All things are possible with God" (Luke 1:37). If God could enable us to make a fifty-state tour without having to sell off our personal belongings and property or go into debt to finance the trip, we knew that with Him anything truly is possible. And as you will see as you read on, there were a number of times when we needed this verse to reassure us. In fact, there were times during the trip when we would repeat this verse over and over to one another, eager to learn how the Lord would resolve a particular situation. The good news is that He never failed us, not even once. He even enabled us to solve what became our "great bicycle dilemma."

David and I slept in the overhead bunk.

Four specially designed bunks with seat belts in the back for the children!

Stored homeschooling books here!

Our RV and Bike Trailer

These signs on the RV got much attention.

Mountains in The Northeast

Boston

Liberty Bell

it all tastes good cooked on a camp stove.

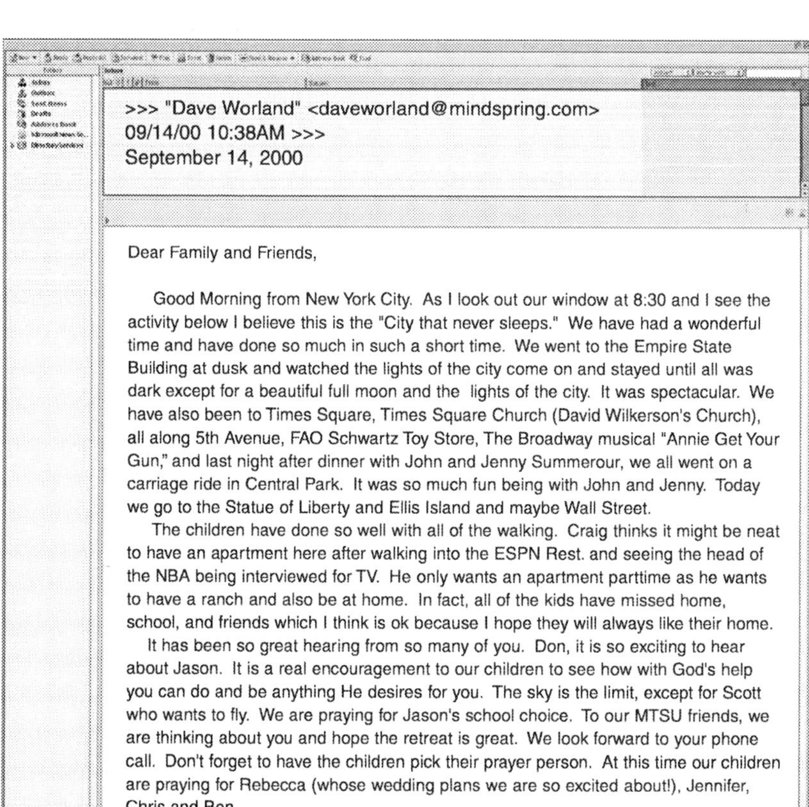

>>> "Dave Worland" <daveworland@mindspring.com>
09/14/00 10:38AM >>>
September 14, 2000

Dear Family and Friends,

Good Morning from New York City. As I look out our window at 8:30 and I see the activity below I believe this is the "City that never sleeps." We have had a wonderful time and have done so much in such a short time. We went to the Empire State Building at dusk and watched the lights of the city come on and stayed until all was dark except for a beautiful full moon and the lights of the city. It was spectacular. We have also been to Times Square, Times Square Church (David Wilkerson's Church), all along 5th Avenue, FAO Schwartz Toy Store, The Broadway musical "Annie Get Your Gun," and last night after dinner with John and Jenny Summerour, we all went on a carriage ride in Central Park. It was so much fun being with John and Jenny. Today we go to the Statue of Liberty and Ellis Island and maybe Wall Street.

The children have done so well with all of the walking. Craig thinks it might be neat to have an apartment here after walking into the ESPN Rest. and seeing the head of the NBA being interviewed for TV. He only wants an apartment parttime as he wants to have a ranch and also be at home. In fact, all of the kids have missed home, school, and friends which I think is ok because I hope they will always like their home.

It has been so great hearing from so many of you. Don, it is so exciting to hear about Jason. It is a real encouragement to our children to see how with God's help you can do and be anything He desires for you. The sky is the limit, except for Scott who wants to fly. We are praying for Jason's school choice. To our MTSU friends, we are thinking about you and hope the retreat is great. We look forward to your phone call. Don't forget to have the children pick their prayer person. At this time our children are praying for Rebecca (whose wedding plans we are so excited about!), Jennifer, Chris and Ben.

To all you teachers, I have always appreciated you, but even have a greater appreciation now after homeschooling. I also see that my children respect your position as the other day at a store, a customer asked me to help her figure out her receipt, and Bonny Jean said, "My mom can do it, she is a teacher!" Suzannah is working hard on her "fonix" (ha, ha)(Phonics) and adjusting to her mom being her teacher.

We are heading to New England, where we will stay near friends and family while David takes two trips to California. Thank you for your prayers. And know we love you all.

If you know anyone that wants to be added to this e-mail, please contact us.

Love, Sally, David, Craig, Scott, Bonny Jean, and Suzannah

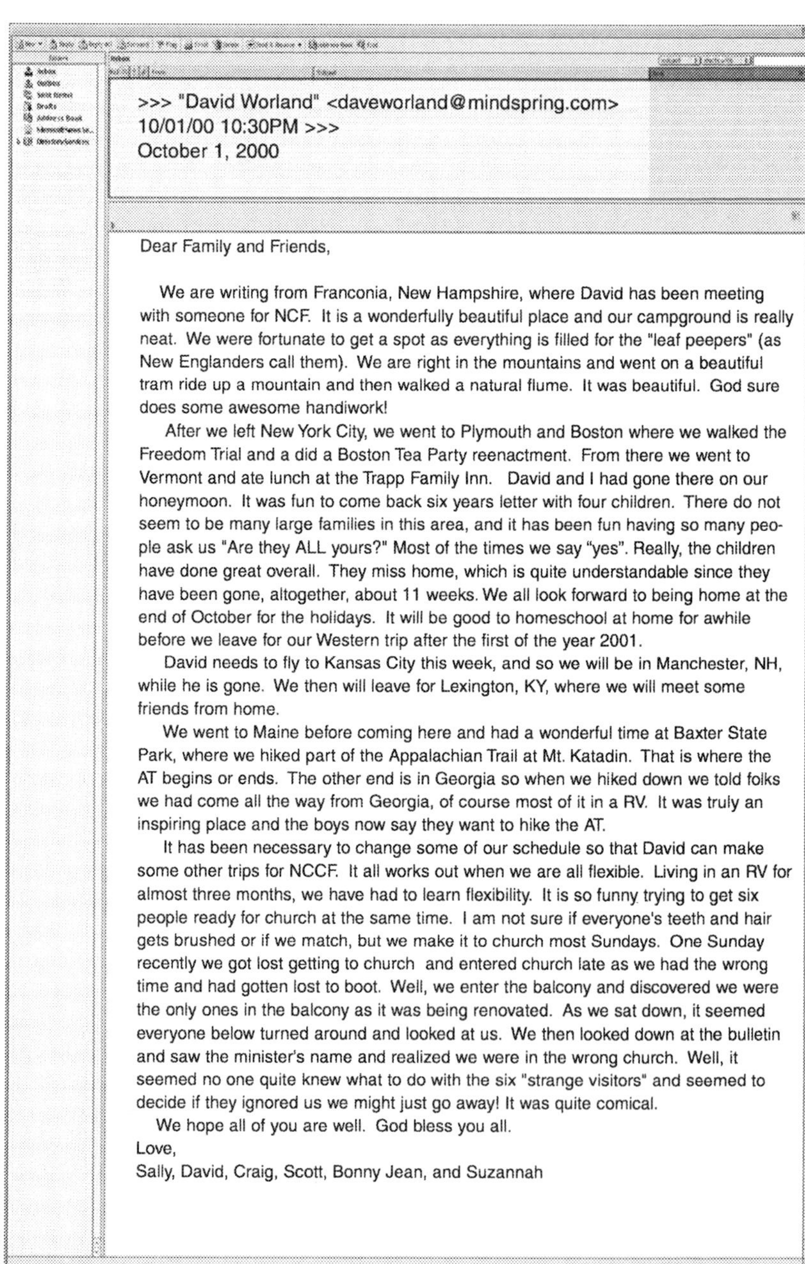

>>> "David Worland" <daveworland@mindspring.com>
10/01/00 10:30PM >>>
October 1, 2000

Dear Family and Friends,

We are writing from Franconia, New Hampshire, where David has been meeting with someone for NCF. It is a wonderfully beautiful place and our campground is really neat. We were fortunate to get a spot as everything is filled for the "leaf peepers" (as New Englanders call them). We are right in the mountains and went on a beautiful tram ride up a mountain and then walked a natural flume. It was beautiful. God sure does some awesome handiwork!

After we left New York City, we went to Plymouth and Boston where we walked the Freedom Trial and a did a Boston Tea Party reenactment. From there we went to Vermont and ate lunch at the Trapp Family Inn. David and I had gone there on our honeymoon. It was fun to come back six years letter with four children. There do not seem to be many large families in this area, and it has been fun having so many people ask us "Are they ALL yours?" Most of the times we say "yes". Really, the children have done great overall. They miss home, which is quite understandable since they have been gone, altogether, about 11 weeks. We all look forward to being home at the end of October for the holidays. It will be good to homeschool at home for awhile before we leave for our Western trip after the first of the year 2001.

David needs to fly to Kansas City this week, and so we will be in Manchester, NH, while he is gone. We then will leave for Lexington, KY, where we will meet some friends from home.

We went to Maine before coming here and had a wonderful time at Baxter State Park, where we hiked part of the Appalachian Trail at Mt. Katadin. That is where the AT begins or ends. The other end is in Georgia so when we hiked down we told folks we had come all the way from Georgia, of course most of it in a RV. It was truly an inspiring place and the boys now say they want to hike the AT.

It has been necessary to change some of our schedule so that David can make some other trips for NCCF. It all works out when we are all flexible. Living in an RV for almost three months, we have had to learn flexibility. It is so funny trying to get six people ready for church at the same time. I am not sure if everyone's teeth and hair gets brushed or if we match, but we make it to church most Sundays. One Sunday recently we got lost getting to church and entered church late as we had the wrong time and had gotten lost to boot. Well, we enter the balcony and discovered we were the only ones in the balcony as it was being renovated. As we sat down, it seemed everyone below turned around and looked at us. We then looked down at the bulletin and saw the minister's name and realized we were in the wrong church. Well, it seemed no one quite knew what to do with the six "strange visitors" and seemed to decide if they ignored us we might just go away! It was quite comical.

We hope all of you are well. God bless you all.

Love,
Sally, David, Craig, Scott, Bonny Jean, and Suzannah

CHAPTER THREE

Road Scholars

Our Little Schoolhouse on the Highway

One of the biggest challenges for our trip would be homeschooling our children. The traveling in itself, and the experiences we would share during that time, would be an education in itself. But even though we were anticipating a unique adventure, life — and formal education — still had to go on.

Even with my college degree in social work, and my years of experience in running summer camps, teaching my children in a homeschool setting — especially while traveling from one state to another — was a daunting responsibility for me. Although David would be able to help somewhat, with everything he had to do to fulfill his work commitments, I knew the task would fall primarily on my shoulders.

I began my preparations by going to some of my friends who homeschooled their children and discussing how they did it. I also went to several bookstores to get books and materials that could provide me with as much insight and understanding as possible about what is required to build a positive homeschool experience. I also spoke with the faculty at our school, Chattanooga Christian, and they were helpful.

One thing we did to encourage the children and reinforce that their education would remain a priority throughout the trip was to have a sign specially made. It read, "We have 4 Road Scholars: Home Schoolers Traveling the U.S.A.," and over the next twelve months it would receive a lot of interesting comments. Once we were approached by some college students who had a look of wonderment. "You have four Rhodes Scholars?" one of them asked. None of the college students, obviously, was a Rhodes Scholar, but we explained what we meant by "4 Road Scholars."

It was very important to me to do a good job with this homeschooling assignment, because I knew our children would be back in a traditional school environment the next year, and their school is very challenging at all grade levels. Since they would return to a very demanding academic schedule, I didn't want any of them to fall behind. While I have always felt great appreciation for men and women who have dedicated their lives to being teachers, my admiration for them soared after my own experience as a homeschool teacher.

Philosophically, I have always felt that one of the hallmarks of an effective parent is consistency. Our trip did nothing to change my thinking on this, but I realized that it's a lot harder as a twenty-four-hour-a-day job, without any breaks. When I got a little frazzled, or the kids and I started to wear on each other, we had to accept we were at school and at home at the same time!

At the start, I had laughingly asked God not to make it necessary for me to teach reading, but because of Suzannah's foreign adoption (chapter six), reading was difficult. With her, my challenge was my combined roles as mom and teacher, because in the orphanage her teacher also had been her caregiver. That had not always been a positive experience for her, and I didn't want her to be confused.

Ultimately, I determined that while I would do the best I could to teach her in any subject, it was most important to just be her mother. When we worked on her reading, I simply took her at a different pace than I did with the other children, letting her learn on her own terms and at her own comfort level.

For Bonny Jean, math has always been most difficult, so we worked hard in that area, especially in learning the multiplication tables. One of my "assignments" with her was just assuring her that she was not dumb at math — but rather that she was very smart and, with hard work, she would be able to do the work very well. Thankfully, after our trip had ended and she returned to the regular school setting, we found she was doing very well in math, so we feel the homeschool experience was very profitable in helping build self-confidence.

I saw the respect my children have for their teachers one day when we were at a store in New Hampshire to pick up a few necessities. One of the customers in the store, looking a bit perplexed at what she had just been charged, asked if I could help her double-check her sales receipt. Spontaneously, Bonny Jean stated, "My mom can do it —she is a teacher!"

During the first part of our trip, I felt very anxious about how well I could do as a homeschool teacher, but over the second part my level of concern lessened as we became more accustomed to a routine, and I settled into my teaching role. It helped also to communicate with my homeschooling friends by e-mail and compare our progress. It was heartening to find out that the children and I were doing quite well.

Homeschooling, I decided early on, would not be limited to specific hours in each day. I took every opportunity I could to teach the children, trying to incorporate what we saw and experienced into some area of their homeschool curriculum. We worked in the RV, in the hotel rooms, at picnic tables, along curbsides, in parking lots, alongside swimming pools — wherever we could and an opportune time presented itself. Sometimes we did this to give David some quiet time to work; other times I just wanted them to have a chance to get outside routine surroundings and enjoy some variety. Obviously, through this process they were able to learn and discover many things they could not have encountered in a traditional classroom.

While we were traveling, each of our children would work on their schoolwork a lot. If I was driving and they had questions, they would individually come up to the passenger seat in front of the RV, and we could discuss particular problems they were having. Sometimes they would just call out to me from the back of the RV and I would respond, but eventually we decided there had to be a better way for learning without having to yell at one another over the noise of the RV. Consequently we purchased a set of walkie-talkies so we could talk back and forth in normal tones. This was fun, and I found it a way to utilize my time while I was occupied only with turning the steering wheel and pushing on the gas pedal.

As much as possible, we tried to complete the children's schoolwork in the mornings. If we were still traveling in the afternoon, to occupy their time we had TVs in the back and in the front (our living room area) so sometimes they could watch videos. The children learned to be very creative, playing lots of games together and doing artwork, as well as doing the obvious — looking out the windows to see the sights and scenery of each state we visited.

Occasionally, the kids would get especially ambitious. It was my practice to prepare lesson plans every evening for the following day, giving the order of what each child needed to accomplish that day. One morning I found out that Craig and Scott had gotten up during the night, found their assignments for the next day in my planner, and completed all their work for the following day before going back to bed.

When I got up the next morning, the boys were still sound asleep but they had left their schoolwork where I could readily see it. Appreciating their initiative, I let the boys enjoy an extended snooze while Bonny Jean and Suzannah went about their typical school day. While I didn't want studying in the wee hours of the morning to become a regular practice, I knew the boys needed to be rewarded, not disciplined, for bending our homeschool rules a bit.

Early in 2001, I assigned each of the children written and oral book reports. It was interesting to see them react as the critical audience for their siblings. They all did well, although brevity was not one of their strong points. The oral presentations were only supposed to be about five minutes each, but it was well over an hour by the time the kids finished giving their talks. David, who had spent a very busy day at the computer and on the phone, later admitted to dozing off twice during the presentations.

Not All Books and Paperwork

Of course, the marvelous education our children received over the course of our travels was more than academic. In our restricted living quarters, we learned a lot about each other — both positive and negative. Discovering the virtues (and necessity) of talking out differences is something that many individuals never learn. We also gained an understanding of what tolerance means, that thinking differently from someone else does not necessarily mean that either of you is wrong — just different.

Traveling through the Northeast on the first stage of our trip — visiting Philadelphia, Washington, D.C., Williamsburg, Virginia, New York City, Boston, and then other parts of New England — definitely was a boost to the homeschooling dynamic of our travels. Going to Gettsyburg, Pennsylvania, for instance, gave us a fresh perspective on the Civil War, even though our home in Chickamauga, Georgia, is mere miles from the site of one of the toughest battles of the War between the States. Knowing how far we had traveled, we gained a new understanding of the scope of the war.

Among our favorite stops in the nation's capital were the Capitol Building, the White House, the Smithsonian Museum, the Washington, Lincoln, and Jefferson Memorials, the Vietnam Memorial, Fords Theatre, and Arlington Cemetery. We could not confirm it, but the boys were thrilled to hear that there supposedly is a basketball court on top of the Supreme Court Building. (Probably for the Justices to practice "slam dunk" legal decisions?)

The Sunday morning we were in Washington, we attended a worship service at the historic New York Avenue Presbyterian Church, where Peter Marshall — who also served as chaplain of the U.S. Senate — had been the pastor. We even sat in the same pew that Abraham Lincoln "rented" while he was President.

One of the great educational benefits of our travels was simplifying the process for memorizing information, such as the names of the U.S. presidents and the order of their succession, as well as the names of the capitals of each state. We saw the birthplaces (or other landmarks) of a number of presidents, and we spent time in many of the state capitals, so we all were able to personalize this information rather than just rely on rote memory.

In Williamsburg, we participated in a special one-week homeschooling event where the kids learned many things about living in colonial times. For instance, they learned about how governmental affairs were conducted, how an old firefighting machine worked, and they even had the opportunity to dress up in clothing of the Williamsburg era. The children didn't seem to think the "stocks" — where people who ran afoul of the law were restrained by having their heads, hands, and feet locked in wooden contraptions — would be a desirable form of discipline these days. Throughout that week, in many respects it was the next best thing to stepping back in time about 200 years.

By the time we arrived in Philadelphia, Pennsylvania, in late August of 2000, we had already put more than 5,000 miles on our RV. We already were learning the meaning of the phrase, "close quarters," but in general things were going very well. We had six different personalities and six different sets of needs to be met, so getting all of us happy at the same time was a challenge, but we had days when that actually happened!

One very practical advantage of traveling in an RV became evident when we found ourselves in the inevitable traffic jam. Once we were stuck in traffic for several hours without moving an inch; there apparently had been an accident up ahead. If we had been in a car or a van, I'm sure our frustration level would have peaked before very long, but we were able to relax and make the best of a bad situation. We made some microwave popcorn, played some games, and even were able to go to the bathroom as needed, while travelers in vehicles all around us were fuming helplessly.

In the City of Brotherly Love, we really felt as if we were stepping back into some of the most momentous days of American history, visiting Independence Hall, the Liberty Bell, and many of the other landmarks that were such an important part of the founding of our country.

New York, One Year Before The Day

Our visit to New York City was fun as well, especially going to the Empire State Building at dusk and watching as the lights of the city came on until they glistened against the night sky. A beautiful full moon added to the spectacular illumination of "the city that never sleeps," as they say. Going to Times Square, David Wilkerson's Times Square Church (made popular in his book, *The Cross and the Switchblade*), walking down Fifth Avenue, touring the FAO Schwartz toy store, and attending the Broadway musical, "Annie Get Your Gun," were unforgettable highlights.

One of my favorite activities was taking an evening carriage ride in Central Park with some good friends from New York City who had come to see us. But for the boys, nothing could top walking into the ESPN Zone Restaurant, where they saw David Stern, the head of the National Basketball Association, being interviewed. Craig decided it would be neat to have an apartment in New York, but only on a part-time basis since he also wants to have a ranch.

However, it wasn't until almost one year later that the reality of our time in New York City hit us in full force. On September 12, 2000, we had taken a ferry across the Hudson River, where we went to the Statue of Liberty and Ellis Island. Nearby the Twin Towers of the World Trade Center had stood proudly. In fact, we have a picture of our entire family standing along the rail of a ferry with the Towers in the background. So, when the attacks occurred on September 11, 2001, like virtually everyone else in the United States, we could not believe it. We remembered the Towers gleaming so brightly in the sun, such wonderful symbols of American creativity, prosperity, and beauty. But suddenly, they were gone, along with thousands of lives of men, women, and children. Once again we realized life on this earth is but a vapor, and we should live with an eternal perspective.

Moving on to Boston and New England continued our ongoing education in the picturesque and historic Northeast. Going to Plymouth, Massachusetts, we were amazed when we saw Plymouth Rock — we had expected to see some huge boulder, but in fact, it's not much more than a rock. It's amazing sometimes how fact doesn't always match up with expectations and imagination.

But in Boston, we walked the Freedom Trail and participated in a Boston Tea Party reenactment, and saw the sobering Holocaust Wall.

Next, we moved on to Vermont, where we got to see some of the Worland family history firsthand: We ate lunch at the Trapp Family Inn, where David and I had gone for our honeymoon almost seventeen years earlier. It was a lot of fun to return there with four children in tow. One interesting thing we noted about that part of the country was that there did not seem to be many large families there. Over and over again, people would ask us, "Are they all yours?" Most of the time we admitted that, yes, they all were ours.

In Maine, we stayed at Baxter State Park, where we walked along part of the Appalachian Trail at Mt. Katadin. This is where this historic trail begins (or ends, depending on how you look at it). Since the other end is in Georgia, as we hiked down the trail we told people we passed that we had come all the way from there. They were really impressed, until we admitted that we had traveled most of that distance in an RV. Our boys, showing more and more of their adventurous spirit, declared that one day they would like to travel the entire Appalachian Trail on foot, from Georgia to Maine. I honestly wouldn't be at all surprised if one day they achieve that desire.

When we arrived in Franconia, New Hampshire, we were fortunate to find a space in a beautiful campground because in early October the "leaf peepers" (as New Englanders call tourists who converge on their region to enjoy the fall colors) had arrived in full force. Once we got settled, we could understand why the area was such an attraction. We rode a tram up a mountain and then walked a natural flume, all the while absorbing the visual tapestry of reds, oranges, yellows, and browns. God sure does some awesome paintings!

Much of our homeschooling over the course of our almost twelve months on the road consisted of material from textbooks we had brought with us, but what we learned firsthand — particularly on this Northeastern swing — couldn't have been duplicated through any book. Over those three months, we experienced in person more history, geography, biology, botany, and social science than many people gain in an entire lifetime.

When the first stage of our trip came to an end at the beginning of November, the timing was perfect. We already had enjoyed so many wonderful experiences, but we all needed a break, especially the kids. By mid-October, they had already started to count down the days until they would be able to again sleep in their own beds and trudge around the familiar surroundings of our "homestead." The children also were eagerly discussing how they were going to decorate for Christmas, realizing how much they love their home and the traditions within its walls.

It had been delightful to rendezvous with friends and family on the road, such as the Tinney family in Kentucky and even my parents, when they met us at the Appalachian Homecoming in Norris, Tennessee, but we were looking forward to getting reconnected with friends and family we had left behind.

For me, my homeschool teaching responsibilities would continue but it would be a nice change of pace to plan our activities in our real home. We knew that in January we would again be taking to the highway, heading west, but for about two months we would be able to satisfy Craig's desire to be "a normal family."

Our stay-at-home break did prove to be therapeutic and when the time came, we were ready to go, as the Willie Nelson song says, "On the Road Again." Our homeschooling experience on the second half of the journey went much more smoothly since we had grown accustomed to the routine, and the kids had gotten used to Teacher Mom. I realized that I was probably learning as much as they were, including the important facts of what is "cool" and what is not.

Camping, Except on a National Scale

Our primary motivation in desiring this trip for our family was not so much to accomplish the feat of being in each of the fifty states, but to give the children a good taste for the excitement of engaging in something new and different. I suppose my love for novel experiences stems from my family background. I grew up the second of four children, with an older sister, Bonny Belle, and two younger brothers, Tommy and Chip. We were raised in the Signal Mountain area of Chattanooga, Tennessee, but educationally it seemed I was always on the move. I attended six elementary schools, one middle school, one high school, and then attended the University of Tennessee Chattanooga and Cleveland State Community College, before settling down long enough to get a degree in social work from Middle Tennessee State University.

Most of my family loved the outdoors and enjoyed camping. There was something inexpressibly wonderful about spending a night in the outdoors, surrounded by the sights, sounds, and smells of the world God created. At the time, I had little notion of how valuable my camping experience would prove to be as my husband, our children, and I launched our cross-country journey many years later.

For some people, the prospect of a trans-U.S.A. excursion with many of the overnights spent in campgrounds would not be appealing. I have a friend who says his idea of "roughing it" is a Holiday Inn with a black-and-white TV — and no cable. And granted, living in an RV was not exactly the same as pitching a tent each night, but I still felt it added to our sense of adventure, always stopping at new places and never being sure what we could expect.

My Childhood Dreams

Along with camping, I grew up loving horses and desperately wanting to have one. One Christmas I told my parents that I didn't want anything except a horse. My parents told me that they could not afford to get me a horse, but I was stubborn (actually, I prefer to describe my attitude as "determined"). Ultimately, my parents agreed to get me a horse that year, but insisted that I had to take personal responsibility for caring for the horse, both in time and expense. So to pay expenses, at the age of fourteen I started to teach horseback riding and also did a lot of babysitting.

Did you ever, at a young age, for some reason "know" you were going to be or do something very specific when you got older? Well, I knew that one day I wanted to run a summer camp. Actually, when I was about fourteen years old, I awakened from a dream in which I believed — and still do, to this day — that God was telling me that one day He wanted me to run a camp for children and somehow combine the camping experience with horses.

At the time, my family and I lived on a two-acre lot on Signal Mountain, Tennessee, just north of Chattanooga. For practice, I would gather my brothers and any neighborhood kids I could get to set up tents in our front yard and simulate an overnight camp. We had all kinds of activities — swimming, identifying birds and leaves, softball on a nearby field, running a camp store (we sold candy bars to neighborhood kids and to each other), and we even had a rest hour.

From that time I began planning for one day owning and operating my own summer day camp, although I kept this ambition a virtual secret for several years. I did mention it to the minister of our church one time, telling him that I felt God had called me to do this, but he scoffed at the idea, commenting, "No, He has called you to be a missionary." I respected my pastor, but felt if that was what God wanted me to do, He would also have told me.

I asked my parents if they could start looking for land that was for sale that might be suitable for a campground. They had often talked about running a resort, so I thought combining our ideas made a lot of sense. Initially, they resisted my suggestion, but after a lot of begging and persuasion (on my part), we started looking at some properties. We found one, about five years later, that seemed ideal near Chickamauga, Georgia, about 17 miles south of Chattanooga.

After I graduated from Middle Tennessee State University in December of 1974, I was hired as youth director for the YWCA in Chattanooga, but I never let go of my dream to run summer camps. To gain experience, I worked at camps in Nashville, Apison and Monterey, Tennessee and then an attorney asked a friend and me to start a resident camp on Monteagle Mountain, about 50 miles north of Chattanooga. It was a tremendous amount of work, but a great learning experience.

In 1976, I finally started my own camp, which I called "Camp Hidden Hollow." Initially, it was not very elaborate, but I did drive and provide transportation for children attending the camp, and planned a variety of fun outdoor experiences for them, such as swimming in the lake and wading in the cool creek, horseback riding, archery, and nature crafts and studies.

Later on, we would start every morning with a brief devotional at the lakeside chapel I helped build. For about as long as I can remember, my relationship with Jesus Christ has been the most important thing in my life, so it just seemed natural to incorporate a spiritual dimension into the camping experience.

So when it came time for us to take to the road, with only enough food for a few meals and having to cook much of the time on an outdoor stove, we were well-prepared. It wasn't quite the same as Lewis & Clark, but in our own way, we were engaged in the exploration of a lifetime. Sometimes, as explained in the next chapter, our search boiled down to the necessities — where to wash our clothes and where to play basketball.

SCHOOLING
takes place
EVERYWHERE!
WE HAVE FOUR
"ROAD SCHOLARS"
HOME SCHOOLERS
TRAVELING THE USA
THE WORLANDS
RECESS

SUZANNAH

>>> "David Worland" <daveworland@mindspring.com>
10/14/00 09:33AM >>>

Dear Family and Friends,

Here we are three months later winding down this first part of our 2000-2001 trip. Our family has now been to 25 states together. We have really seen a lot of most of these states as we stayed several days and have crisscrossed back and forth for Dave's meetings. I am truly thankful that we have been allowed this unique opportunity. What a marvelous education for our four children. We have learned so much about each other (positive and negative). We have had to be willing to talk out differences and to learn that thinking differently than someone else does not make you wrong. Craig and Scott have both had birthdays on this trip, and so they are now 13 and 12. We are learning all kinds of new thought patterns as well as speech! WHATEVER!

We are in Pigeon Forge, Tennessee, now and stayed in a motel with an indoor water slide that is 100 feet long. The children and I all swam last night and had a ball. I realize that I have a lot of kid in me when I heard another mother reprimanding some children for doing something I thought was fun. Oh well, I have always said I wanted the children to enjoy being children and not grow up too fast, and I must be that example!

We are all looking forward to being at home and to sleeping in our own beds. We have some more trips that we will need to make in the next couple of months, but for the most part, we will be at home until we leave in January for our Western trip. I am looking forward to homeschooling at home for awhile. The children are already talking about how they are going to decorate for Christmas. They have really realized how much they love home.

Thank you for your fun responses to our e-mails. We are sorry we haven't been able to respond individually but it is difficult to find places from which to e-mail.

By the way, we had a marvelous time meeting the Tinney family in Kentucky and my parents later at the Appalachian Homecoming in Norris, Tenn.

David has really been working hard to get ready for the Christian Church and Community Foundation Conference in Atlanta next week. Sometimes we think his cell phone is glued to his ear! He has also had to fly several different places for meetings, and the kids and I have learned we can make it on our own in a strange (to us) city. We have met some really nice people associated with David's work, which has been really neat.

Take care and God bless each of you.

Love,

Sally, David, Craig, Scott, Bonny Jean, and Suzannah

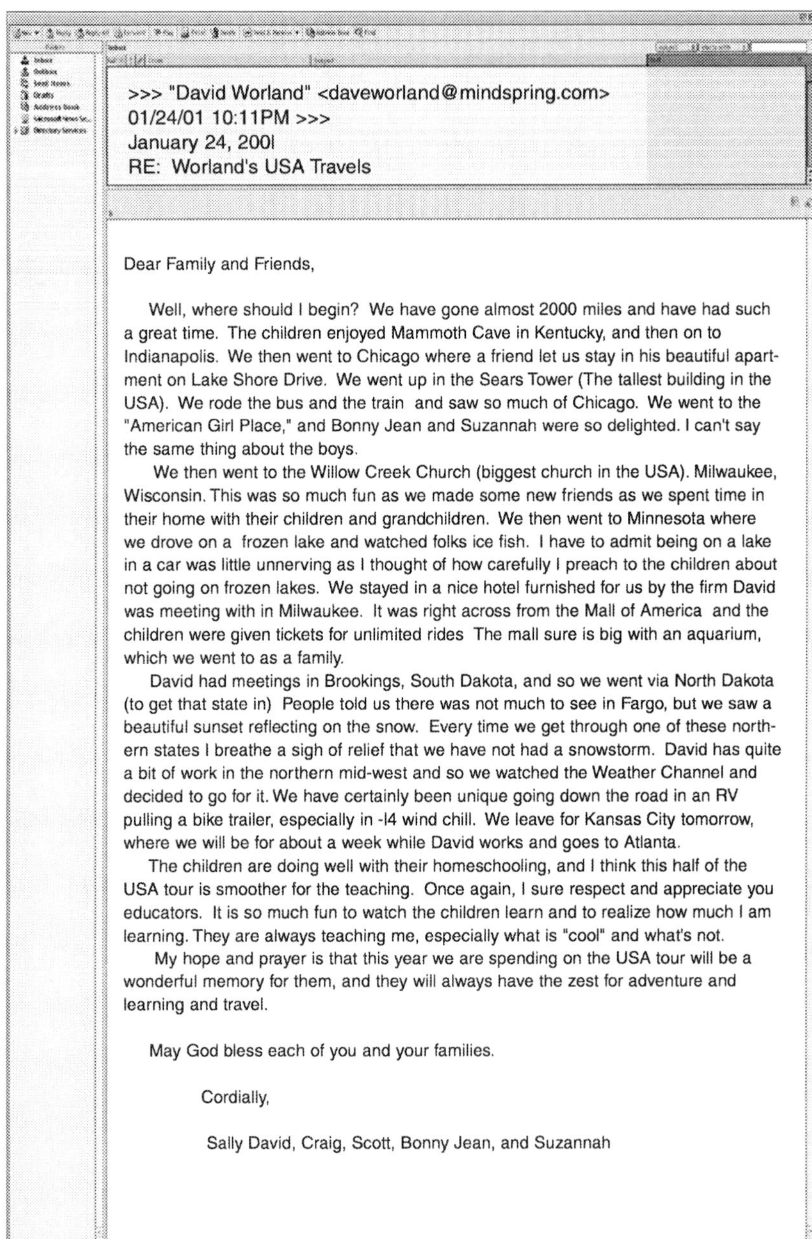

>>> "David Worland" <daveworland@mindspring.com>
01/24/01 10:11PM >>>
January 24, 2001
RE: Worland's USA Travels

Dear Family and Friends,

Well, where should I begin? We have gone almost 2000 miles and have had such a great time. The children enjoyed Mammoth Cave in Kentucky, and then on to Indianapolis. We then went to Chicago where a friend let us stay in his beautiful apartment on Lake Shore Drive. We went up in the Sears Tower (The tallest building in the USA). We rode the bus and the train and saw so much of Chicago. We went to the "American Girl Place," and Bonny Jean and Suzannah were so delighted. I can't say the same thing about the boys.

We then went to the Willow Creek Church (biggest church in the USA). Milwaukee, Wisconsin. This was so much fun as we made some new friends as we spent time in their home with their children and grandchildren. We then went to Minnesota where we drove on a frozen lake and watched folks ice fish. I have to admit being on a lake in a car was little unnerving as I thought of how carefully I preach to the children about not going on frozen lakes. We stayed in a nice hotel furnished for us by the firm David was meeting with in Milwaukee. It was right across from the Mall of America and the children were given tickets for unlimited rides The mall sure is big with an aquarium, which we went to as a family.

David had meetings in Brookings, South Dakota, and so we went via North Dakota (to get that state in) People told us there was not much to see in Fargo, but we saw a beautiful sunset reflecting on the snow. Every time we get through one of these northern states I breathe a sigh of relief that we have not had a snowstorm. David has quite a bit of work in the northern mid-west and so we watched the Weather Channel and decided to go for it. We have certainly been unique going down the road in an RV pulling a bike trailer, especially in -14 wind chill. We leave for Kansas City tomorrow, where we will be for about a week while David works and goes to Atlanta.

The children are doing well with their homeschooling, and I think this half of the USA tour is smoother for the teaching. Once again, I sure respect and appreciate you educators. It is so much fun to watch the children learn and to realize how much I am learning. They are always teaching me, especially what is "cool" and what's not.

My hope and prayer is that this year we are spending on the USA tour will be a wonderful memory for them, and they will always have the zest for adventure and learning and travel.

May God bless each of you and your families.

Cordially,

Sally David, Craig, Scott, Bonny Jean, and Suzannah

CHAPTER FOUR

"Where's the Nearest Basketball Hoop?"

Even in the friendly, familiar confines of home, challenges inevitably crop up. Appliances fail, things get misplaced, schedules become disrupted, etc. In fact, there are times when Murphy's first law, "If something can go wrong, it will," seems branded on the roof of the house. So you can imagine the challenges you encounter while transporting a family of six from state to state, going places where you have never been.

Living in the normal, stationary house with all the typical conveniences readily available, it's easy to take them for granted. But after living in an RV equipped with just the essentials for safe, efficient travel, it's amazing the kinds of common things you learn to appreciate — Things like washing machines and basketball hoops.

Often when we would conclude a day's travel and arrive at a camping ground or a hotel, two of the first questions we asked the people managing the facility were, "Do you have a place to play basketball?" and "Do you have a laundromat?"

Our ability to keep our clothes laundered, given that individual wardrobes were so limited, became a matter of special urgency. While the rest of the family would head off to investigate the extent and quality of recreational facilities, David and I would gather up our dirty clothes in search of the "laundrymat." Today, quarters have become popular because of the special statehood coins that so many people have started to collect. But I learned how important plain old quarters are when it became necessary to visit coin-operated laundromats so often. I can't even guess how many George Washington-faced quarters I stuffed in the washing machines and dryers during our approximately one-year adventure.

With our self-imposed once-a-week rotation of seven outfits, we wore our clothes so often that they eventually began to look threadbare. Forget designer logos! It got to the point that we were just thankful for any brand of clean socks (without holes).

From the boys' perspective, finding a basketball goal was every bit as critical as finding somewhere for me to wash clothes. They didn't want their "hoop skills" to diminish at all during their time away from home. At one of our stops, they actually met a young man who played basketball for the University of Syracuse and prevailed upon him to play a game with them.

On one occasion when we were frantically and fruitlessly searching for somewhere that they could play basketball, I suggested that maybe I get a peach basket to hang on the RV for them. That was how I first played basketball and after all, that is how James Naismith started the game of basketball. But for some reason, the boys didn't warm to the peach basket idea — they had to have the traditional metal hoops, preferably with net to catch the ball as it swished through.

Occasionally, we would find facilities that were just perfect for the kids. For instance, in Kansas City, Missouri, we found a community center that offered day passes. It had a large swimming pool with slides, rivers, vortex pools, and a playground right in the water. For the boys, the center had a gym where they spent hours practicing basketball. Craig and Scott were even brazen enough to ask adults who were playing a pickup basketball game if they could join them. Initially, they received a firm "No," but they persisted — "persistence neutralizes resistance" the old saying goes — and finally they were allowed to play and show that they were "worthy" of playing competitive ball.

After all those days of being confined in the RV, the kids even had a chance to "climb the wall" at the center. There was a wonderful climbing wall, complete with handholds and footholds, and Bonny Jean and Scott had a great time clambering to the top over and over again.

Occasional Second Thoughts

As an adult who had dreamed and prayed about this trip for so many years, I never once wondered why we had undertaken such an ambitious endeavor. To me, it was just a gift from God, something that He wanted us to do. Yes, I often missed my own washing machine and the other conveniences of home, and sometimes my role in caring for the family seemed a bit overwhelming. But part of that was simply due to expectations I had set for myself. I felt I needed to get everything done right, and that each of the kids had to be taught properly.

I also felt it was my responsibility to make sure that everyone was happy, wanting to free David up as much as possible so he could concentrate on his work. I wanted to make sure that he was not hindered in any way in completing his work at the high level of excellence he expects of himself. So if it seemed there was too much friction among the kids, or if they weren't acting as cohesively as I wanted them to be, somehow I chose to assume responsibility. Being peacekeeper and happiness broker certainly was a role I should never have taken on because no one can be responsible for someone else's happiness. Eventually, I came to terms with the reality that I didn't need to put myself under that kind of stress.

There were times when I didn't relish my role as primary supervisor of the kids, especially if it had been a hard day and I wasn't feeling all that great myself. But then I would remind myself that my dream of taking my family on a tour of the United States was only possible because of the work David was doing.

At the same time, while David fully agreed that our trip was God ordained, it was definitely harder for him to travel with the entire family and remain focused on all the work he had to do. During the first half of the trip, he commented a few times that he wasn't certain that the Foundation would be able to send us back for the second half of the trip, but for me there was never a doubt. The way I looked at it, if God had planned this, then He would take care of all the details. As it turned out, there was never a time when we seriously had to face a possibility of not completing our trip.

There were times during our journey when the children would openly wonder if it was worth it. The boys especially, on several occasions, made comments that they didn't want to travel anymore, that they felt as if the trip wasn't the best thing for them and that they wanted to go home. Both Craig and Scott, at one time or another, said things like, "This is the dumbest thing we have ever done!" or "Here I am, missing out on basketball and missing out on being with my friends." But then the next day something special would happen and their attitudes would perk up dramatically. It would be gratifying then to hear them say, "You know, this is pretty cool," letting us know that despite their occasional grumbling, they were in this adventure with us for the long haul.

The girls, being more relational, also had times when they felt homesick, sometimes to the point of shedding tears. One particular day we were leaving Mississippi and crossing the Mississippi River into Memphis, Tennessee, so we could show the children the famous mallard ducks at the historic Peabody Hotel. As we passed the Tennessee state line, I could see the brainstorm brewing in Suzannah's mind.

"Mom, we're in Tennessee!" she said, having no idea where Memphis was located in relation to the rest of the state. "Tennessee is where we go to school. Can't we go home for the night and get some new clothes, and then we can come back?" She didn't understand that Memphis is more than 300 miles and an ambitious drive of more than six hours to our home near Chattanooga.

David and I laughed, and I agreed with Suzannah that it would be nice to get some new clothes to wear. But we assured our daughter that unfortunately, a "quick trip" back home was not an option for us.

As I recount our experiences, there is one point that I hope comes across very clearly. The Worlands are definitely not the perfect family — and we certainly don't have it all together. This trip even magnified our many imperfections.

We had as many disagreements as any family would during our sojourn, even over where we would go to eat. Some time into the first part of our trip, David and I reached the conclusion that a cross-country U.S.A. trip should not be conducted as a democracy. Initially, we had thought it would be nice to let the children choose which restaurant we should visit, especially because when we are home, we rarely go out to eat. But for the second half of the trip we dispensed with that notion. It put too much pressure on us and often the simple selection of an eating place would lead to a heated debate. Food isn't worth that much conflict!

The "Get Ready for Church" Maneuvers

One of the more challenging aspects of our journey was the maneuvering needed for all of us to get dressed for a special occasion, including Sunday mornings when it was time to get ready for church. For six people to get their hair done, teeth brushed, clothes on, stockings and tights on, and shoes on — and make sure everything matched — was quite the experience. We were glad this occurred only once a week, but it did teach us some valuable lessons in flexibility.

Most of the time we would get the children ready first, one by one. Then, as I declared, "I can't get dressed and do everything I need to do with this many people in this RV!" David and I would usher them out the door charging them to amuse themselves, hoping they would stay clean until it was time for all of us to leave for church.

Suzannah, being the youngest, invariably would find some intriguing objects to pick up or to throw, and would end up getting a little dusty or dirty. But since our good "Sunday goin' to meeting" clothes were included in our seven-outfits-a-week wardrobe, she had to make do. After a while, she learned the importance of restraining her energy and keeping clean while the adults finished getting ready.

Some Sundays proved to be more hectic than others. One particular morning, after rushing around with one eye warily watching the clock, we lost our way to the church we had chosen to attend. When we finally arrived at the worship center, the service already was well underway, but we went in anyway. Not wanting to cause a disturbance, we all climbed to the balcony, only to find we were the only ones up there since it was being renovated. Even though we had tried to keep quiet, it seemed as if everyone in the sanctuary below turned to stare at us.

It was only then that we looked down at the bulletin and saw the minister's name and realized that not only were we late, but we also had arrived at the wrong church. It was too late to do anything, however, so we remained until the conclusion of the service. The regular members seemed uncertain what to do about our unexpected appearance on the scene, so apparently they had decided that if they ignored us, we might just go away. That is exactly what we did, as soon as the last note of the closing hymn ended.

Not So Wide, Open Spaces

To enable David to focus on his work responsibilities, I served as the primary chauffeur and it worked out very well. While driving, I could focus on the ever-changing scenery as the miles whizzed by.

When the children needed discipline, David often became the one called upon to administer what was needed. Unfortunately, when he became immersed in his work and had his earphones on, he often couldn't hear what was going on around him, and I would ignore the chaos behind me unless it became unreasonable. A few times he commented that perhaps we should have tried to find a screen like they have in police cars so the kids couldn't hear us, and we couldn't hear them.

Living and traveling together was good for teaching us how to handle conflict promptly, as it arose. When you're riding together in an RV, there is no such thing as stepping outside to cool off or fleeing to the privacy of your own room. We quickly learned that we just couldn't get mad at each other and refuse to talk about it — because we simply couldn't stand it. We were too closed up for too long not to interact or acknowledge to one another if something was bothering us. We had no choice but to learn how to talk out our differences more effectively than we had been doing before we started our trip.

Yes, our very normal Worland girls would have their screaming matches, and the boys would engage in their physical tussles. As hard as we tried, we could not always apply the admonition from the Bible, "In your anger, do not sin" (Ephesians 4:26).

There were those moments when one or the other of us felt that conflict could be much more easily avoided if there only were fewer of us to cause friction. One evening when we were in Yellowstone National Park, Craig, Scott, and Suzannah had all disappeared from our sight as they explored the wonders of that natural treasure. Only Bonny Jean, then ten years old, had remained in the RV with David and me. She has a very interesting way about her — even though she fits in very nicely with our other three children. I have felt for a long time she, for one, would have done just fine without any siblings (at least for a short while).

It was growing dark, and David and I increasingly were feeling typical parental concern. We knew that the park was home to bears, mountain lions, and all kinds of other animals — many of them dangerous — and the disappearing sunlight could increase the children's exposure to peril. We drove all around the park, looking for the kids, blowing the car horn with a special signal meaning that we were searching for missing members of the family. We stopped and asked other tourists if they possibly might have seen two little boys and a little girl walking around together.

The worry on both David's and my faces must have shown, because Bonny Jean took that opportunity to melt the tension by observing, "So this is what it feels like to be an only child!"

Not long afterward, we located the other three and they were perfectly all right, actually oblivious to the anxiety they had been creating for their parents. They had walked a considerable distance from where we had parked and, ignoring the encroaching darkness, had become engrossed in some of the fascinating sights — living and inanimate — that Yellowstone National Park presented to them. The adventuresome threesome collected more information to deposit into their memory banks, and Bonny Jean discovered that even with two brothers and one sister, there are fleeting occasions when you can enjoy being an only child.

Please Don't Feed the...Children

One evening, we all dragged back to the RV after a day of attempting to pack in as much activity as possible during one of David's rare nonworking days. As he and I walked through the door, he made a comment that caught me by surprise: "Don't feed the kids." I looked at him as if to say, "What in the world are you talking about?" David shrugged his shoulders and pointed out, "Well, I've noticed that the children will be winding down and not very energetic, but then we feed them and suddenly they become like the Energizer bunny, full of energy and ready to go again."

I understood what David was getting at, since in our tired physical state we didn't want the kids bouncing off the walls when it was time to go to bed. But after quickly reviewing what I knew about child welfare laws — and the fundamental principles of what is required of a loving, nurturing parent — I concluded that we better not do as David had suggested. We did choose to give them food that was nutritional, but at the same time relatively low in sugar content. At bedtime, I think it's good to hold to a simple philosophy: *Don't starve the kids, but don't stir them up either!*

At nights when we would go to bed, our motorhome was certainly cozy. Since we were all sleeping within close proximity, we could hear everyone else breathing. When someone would turn on his or her bed, the entire RV would shake to reflect the movement. This gave us some degree of understanding of what it must be like to live in countries where families don't have spacious homes with separate rooms for each child that many of us in the U.S.A. and other Western nations enjoy.

On those occasions when we were able to stay in hotels, we usually got either two rooms or a suite so we would not be too cramped together. Usually, the boys would share a bed, and the girls would share another. To give them a treat, occasionally, we would rent two rollaways so everyone could have his or her own bed. In the RV, of course, they each had their own bunk bed, but having their own, independent bed in a hotel room made them so excited. It was as if they had a slice of heaven!

But God had a way of reminding us that we weren't yet as close to heaven as we might have felt at times. While we were in Phoenix, Arizona, David participated in the "Generous Giving" Conference that was being held at the Ritz Carlton Hotel. The annual event attracts many of the most generous philanthropists from around the United States and even from other parts of the world. Because of their stature — and their affluent lifestyles — staying in a place like the Ritz Carlton is not anything out of the norm.

During that weekend, however, the Worland family stayed at the Residence Inn, by Marriott, it was very nice but not to be confused with the Ritz Carlton. We would drive David to his meetings each morning in the RV, drop him off — calling him "Mr. Worland" — and then drive past all the Porsches and Jaguars on our way back to the Residence Inn.

But we did not resent the different accommodations in any way. While David was enjoying the time at the conference, meeting some really wonderful folks, the kids and I had every bit as much fun at our motel. It had the prerequisite basketball court, an outdoor swimming pool, and a court for a modified version of tennis. We did appreciate being able to spend some time apart from the RV. It was a real treat, and we realized that affluence really is a relative commodity.

It's Always Something!

Gilda Radner, who created the character Roseann Roseannadanna on the TV comedy show "Saturday Night Live!" always used a pet phrase to describe the unexpected: "It's always something!" As we traveled, we could have employed that saying a number of times ourselves.

For instance, we were in Stillwater, Minnesota, visiting with friends Ken and Ardie Johnson, when we first experienced problems with the slide-out section of the RV. David was showing Ken how the expandable section worked, but then it wouldn't go back in. There was obviously no way we could head down the highway with this sticking out the side. Ken and David shoved, pushed, maneuvered, and turned the slide-out every way they could think of until they finally coaxed it into going back in, but we wound up having to find someone to fix it so the problem wouldn't occur again.

Then there were times when we felt as if we were victims of the Pony Express. As I explained in an earlier chapter, we had arranged for our mail through a commercial mailing service. According to a predetermined schedule, they were instructed to forward our mail to a specific location so that when we arrived in that city, the mail would be waiting for us. Much of the time, this worked fairly well, but sometimes — too often for our needs and liking — our mail got delayed or misdirected as it was forwarded, so it would have to chase us to our next pickup destination. Finally, after several such snafus, we decided it would be best just to have the mail forwarded by overnight mail, even though it cost us a lot more. It was the only way we could be assured of receiving critical mail on time.

One reason this was so critical was because of my summer camp. I wanted to make sure we received the registration for each child so when we held the camp again in June 2001, every youngster would be expected and accommodated.

Another issue that arose was the need for me to complete our corporate Federal tax return for the camp by March. I had incorrectly understood that the return was not due until May (after we finished our trip), but since it was due in March, I had to scramble to get all the bank statements together and coordinate all of this with our CPA back home. We realized that trying to do business from the road is certainly not as easy as having a fixed setting for it, where you have a place for everything and everything is in its place.

Becoming Old Hands in New Cities

Another lesson we learned was that we could make it on our own in a strange city. Occasionally, when David would have to fly to other cities for meetings or conferences, we would remain behind and "check things out" a little bit more until he returned and then we would set off again. Each child learned how to read a map and was capable of going into a gas station and asking for directions. Discovering how to find our way around in a place we had never been before is something the children will never forget.

By the middle of October, the first three months of our 2000-2001 U.S.A. tour was winding down, and we already had been in twenty-five states, spending at least several days in most of them as we criss-crossed from one city to another for David's meetings.

Lancaster, Pennsylvania
AMISH COUNTRY

We kept the Park Rangers busy.

Bonny Jean in corn field with amish doll.

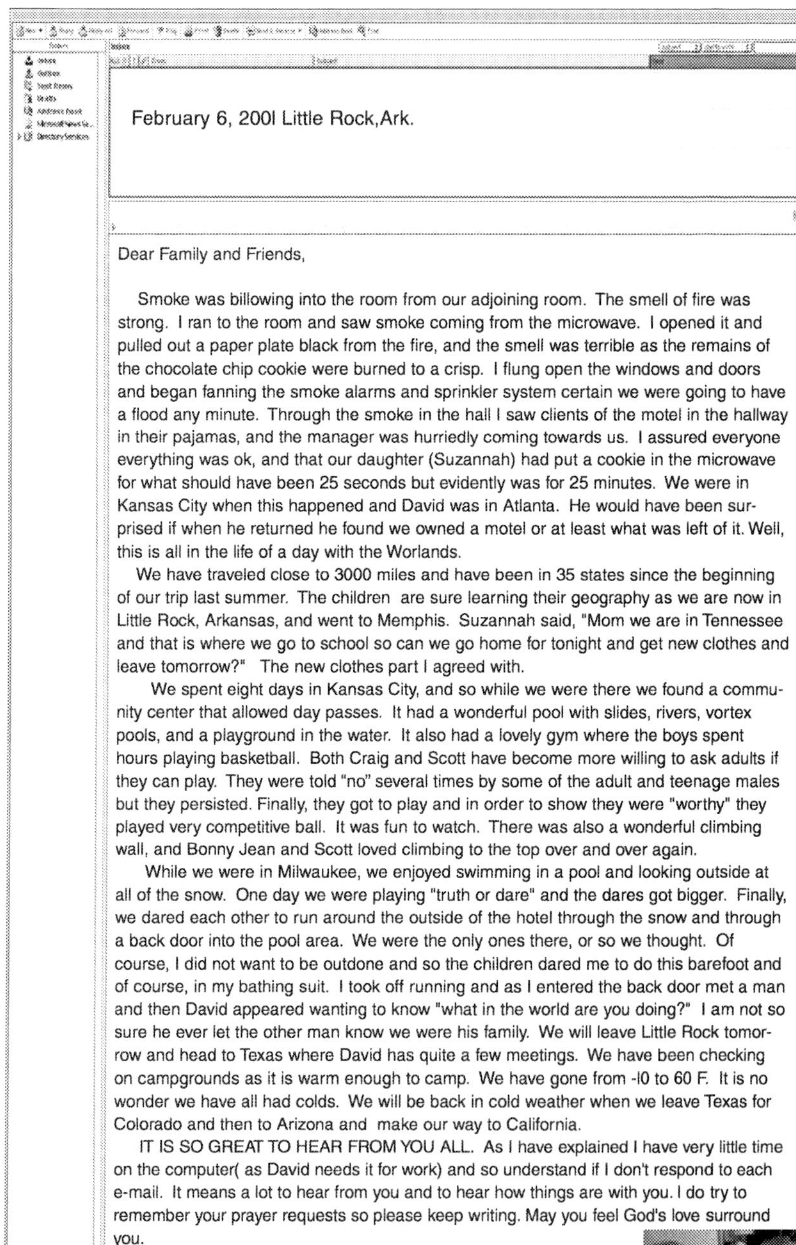

February 6, 2001 Little Rock,Ark.

Dear Family and Friends,

Smoke was billowing into the room from our adjoining room. The smell of fire was strong. I ran to the room and saw smoke coming from the microwave. I opened it and pulled out a paper plate black from the fire, and the smell was terrible as the remains of the chocolate chip cookie were burned to a crisp. I flung open the windows and doors and began fanning the smoke alarms and sprinkler system certain we were going to have a flood any minute. Through the smoke in the hall I saw clients of the motel in the hallway in their pajamas, and the manager was hurriedly coming towards us. I assured everyone everything was ok, and that our daughter (Suzannah) had put a cookie in the microwave for what should have been 25 seconds but evidently was for 25 minutes. We were in Kansas City when this happened and David was in Atlanta. He would have been surprised if when he returned he found we owned a motel or at least what was left of it. Well, this is all in the life of a day with the Worlands.

We have traveled close to 3000 miles and have been in 35 states since the beginning of our trip last summer. The children are sure learning their geography as we are now in Little Rock, Arkansas, and went to Memphis. Suzannah said, "Mom we are in Tennessee and that is where we go to school so can we go home for tonight and get new clothes and leave tomorrow?" The new clothes part I agreed with.

We spent eight days in Kansas City, and so while we were there we found a community center that allowed day passes. It had a wonderful pool with slides, rivers, vortex pools, and a playground in the water. It also had a lovely gym where the boys spent hours playing basketball. Both Craig and Scott have become more willing to ask adults if they can play. They were told "no" several times by some of the adult and teenage males but they persisted. Finally, they got to play and in order to show they were "worthy" they played very competitive ball. It was fun to watch. There was also a wonderful climbing wall, and Bonny Jean and Scott loved climbing to the top over and over again.

While we were in Milwaukee, we enjoyed swimming in a pool and looking outside at all of the snow. One day we were playing "truth or dare" and the dares got bigger. Finally, we dared each other to run around the outside of the hotel through the snow and through a back door into the pool area. We were the only ones there, or so we thought. Of course, I did not want to be outdone and so the children dared me to do this barefoot and of course, in my bathing suit. I took off running and as I entered the back door met a man and then David appeared wanting to know "what in the world are you doing?" I am not so sure he ever let the other man know we were his family. We will leave Little Rock tomorrow and head to Texas where David has quite a few meetings. We have been checking on campgrounds as it is warm enough to camp. We have gone from -10 to 60 F. It is no wonder we have all had colds. We will be back in cold weather when we leave Texas for Colorado and then to Arizona and make our way to California.

IT IS SO GREAT TO HEAR FROM YOU ALL. As I have explained I have very little time on the computer(as David needs it for work) and so understand if I don't respond to each e-mail. It means a lot to hear from you and to hear how things are with you. I do try to remember your prayer requests so please keep writing. May you feel God's love surround you.

With Love, Sally

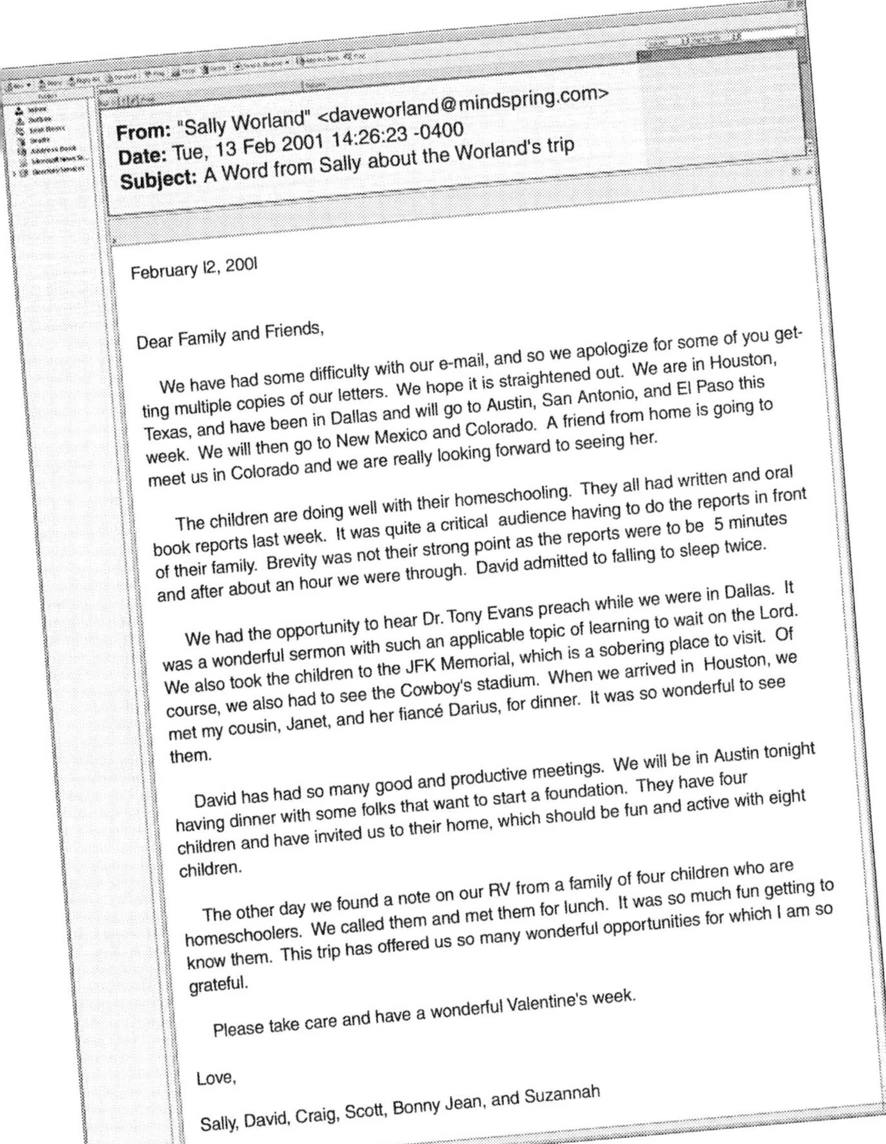

From: "Sally Worland" <daveworland@mindspring.com>
Date: Tue, 13 Feb 2001 14:26:23 -0400
Subject: A Word from Sally about the Worland's trip

February 12, 2001

Dear Family and Friends,

We have had some difficulty with our e-mail, and so we apologize for some of you getting multiple copies of our letters. We hope it is straightened out. We are in Houston, Texas, and have been in Dallas and will go to Austin, San Antonio, and El Paso this week. We will then go to New Mexico and Colorado. A friend from home is going to meet us in Colorado and we are really looking forward to seeing her.

The children are doing well with their homeschooling. They all had written and oral book reports last week. It was quite a critical audience having to do the reports in front of their family. Brevity was not their strong point as the reports were to be 5 minutes and after about an hour we were through. David admitted to falling to sleep twice.

We had the opportunity to hear Dr. Tony Evans preach while we were in Dallas. It was a wonderful sermon with such an applicable topic of learning to wait on the Lord. We also took the children to the JFK Memorial, which is a sobering place to visit. Of course, we also had to see the Cowboy's stadium. When we arrived in Houston, we met my cousin, Janet, and her fiancé Darius, for dinner. It was so wonderful to see them.

David has had so many good and productive meetings. We will be in Austin tonight having dinner with some folks that want to start a foundation. They have four children and have invited us to their home, which should be fun and active with eight children.

The other day we found a note on our RV from a family of four children who are homeschoolers. We called them and met them for lunch. It was so much fun getting to know them. This trip has offered us so many wonderful opportunities for which I am so grateful.

Please take care and have a wonderful Valentine's week.

Love,

Sally, David, Craig, Scott, Bonny Jean, and Suzannah

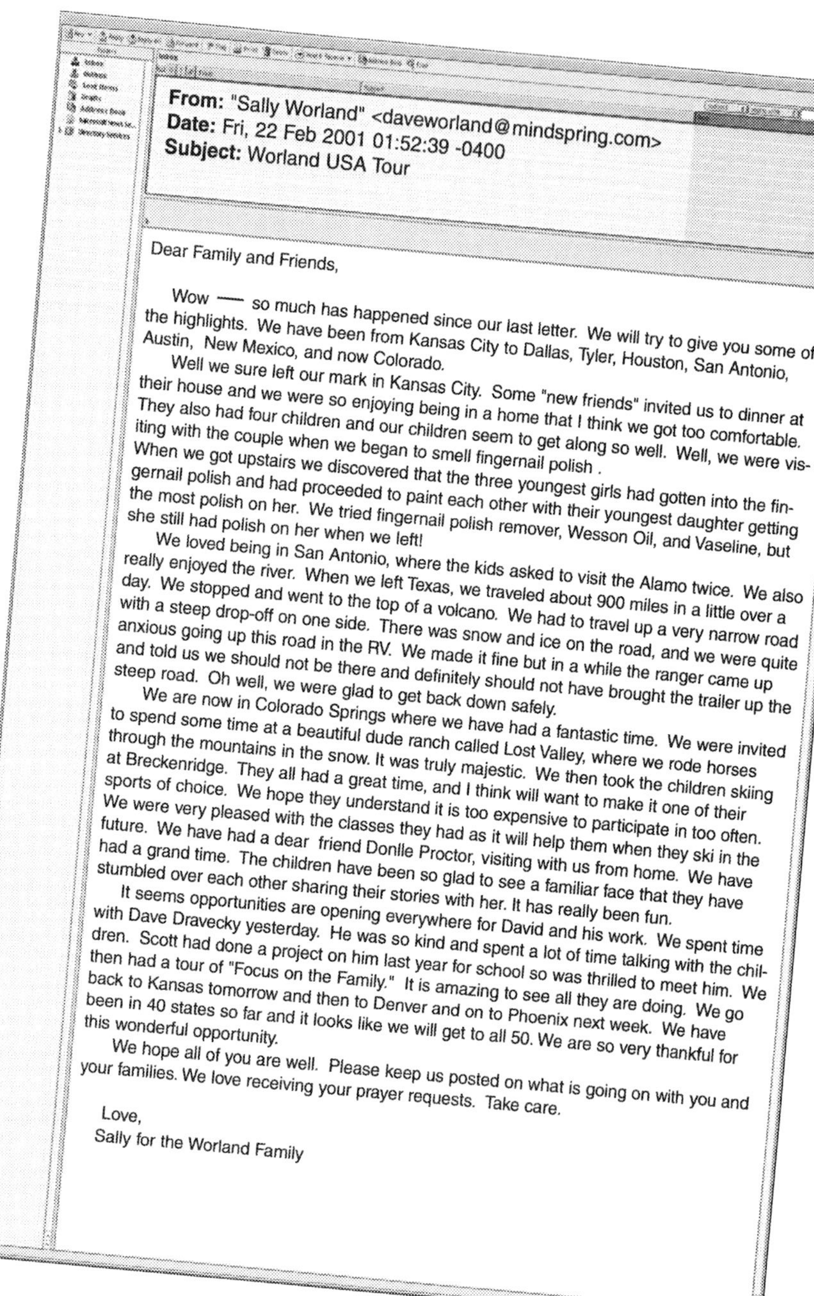

From: "Sally Worland" <daveworland@mindspring.com>
Date: Fri, 22 Feb 2001 01:52:39 -0400
Subject: Worland USA Tour

Dear Family and Friends,

Wow — so much has happened since our last letter. We will try to give you some of the highlights. We have been from Kansas City to Dallas, Tyler, Houston, San Antonio, Austin, New Mexico, and now Colorado.

Well we sure left our mark in Kansas City. Some "new friends" invited us to dinner at their house and we were so enjoying being in a home that I think we got too comfortable. They also had four children and our children seem to get along so well. Well, we were visiting with the couple when we began to smell fingernail polish . When we got upstairs we discovered that the three youngest girls had gotten into the fingernail polish and had proceeded to paint each other with their youngest daughter getting the most polish on her. We tried fingernail polish remover, Wesson Oil, and Vaseline, but she still had polish on her when we left!

We loved being in San Antonio, where the kids asked to visit the Alamo twice. We also really enjoyed the river. When we left Texas, we traveled about 900 miles in a little over a day. We stopped and went to the top of a volcano. We had to travel up a very narrow road with a steep drop-off on one side. There was snow and ice on the road, and we were quite anxious going up this road in the RV. We made it fine but in a while the ranger came up and told us we should not be there and definitely should not have brought the trailer up the steep road. Oh well, we were glad to get back down safely.

We are now in Colorado Springs where we have had a fantastic time. We were invited to spend some time at a beautiful dude ranch called Lost Valley, where we rode horses through the mountains in the snow. It was truly majestic. We then took the children skiing at Breckenridge. They all had a great time, and I think will want to make it one of their sports of choice. We hope they understand it is too expensive to participate in too often. We were very pleased with the classes they had as it will help them when they ski in the future. We have had a dear friend Donlle Proctor, visiting with us from home. We have had a grand time. The children have been so glad to see a familiar face that they have stumbled over each other sharing their stories with her. It has really been fun.

It seems opportunities are opening everywhere for David and his work. We spent time with Dave Dravecky yesterday. He was so kind and spent a lot of time talking with the children. Scott had done a project on him last year for school so was thrilled to meet him. We then had a tour of "Focus on the Family." It is amazing to see all they are doing. We go back to Kansas tomorrow and then to Denver and on to Phoenix next week. We have been in 40 states so far and it looks like we will get to all 50. We are so very thankful for this wonderful opportunity.

We hope all of you are well. Please keep us posted on what is going on with you and your families. We love receiving your prayer requests. Take care.

Love,
Sally for the Worland Family

CHAPTER FIVE

"Are We Going to the Mountain With the Heads in it?"

Since I had already visited each of the fifty states myself, it was fun to experience this second go-round through the eyes of my children. This gave me an appreciation for each one's uniqueness, and also helped me to see the attractions of each state from four very special perspectives.

For instance, when we were headed for South Dakota, Bonny Jean (who was nine years old when we started the trip and turned ten during it) suddenly got a big smile on her face and asked, "Are we going to the mountain with the heads in it?" Of course, she was referring to Mount Rushmore near Rapid City, South Dakota, featuring the faces of four presidents sculpted in stone, but to her it was the mountain with the heads in it. Why not?

Earlier in our trip, we had seen another "mountain with a head in it" — actually, the so-called Man in the Mountain in New Hampshire, which if viewed from a certain angle seems to contain the striking profile of a man. It was interesting to discover how often people kept cropping up in the rocks across America.

Our time at Mt. Rushmore marked another of our recurring encounters with park rangers. On this occasion, the ranger simply reprimanded us for parking in the wrong place. Thankfully, he didn't see our energetic young ones climbing the rocks right behind him, or we all may have ended up in the clinker. I like to think that the reason we drew so much attention from park rangers was not that we were always doing things that were very out of line. But frankly, a family of six in an RV pulling a trailer with six bicycles that shows up at a state or national park during the off-season can be fairly conspicuous especially when the door of the RV reads, "Four Road Scholars: Home Schoolers Traveling the U.S.A."

Hearing the dramatic story of how Mt. Rushmore was created was amazing, especially since we could look at the magnificent carvings of George Washington, Abraham Lincoln, Thomas Jefferson, and Theodore Roosevelt and imagine men crawling all over the mountain, sometimes carefully placing dynamite charges to remove unwanted rock and other times chiseling away rock to put in the fine details of the great presidents' faces.

Throughout our trip, we were struck with the variety we found even among the mountains — the Great Smoky Mountains, the Appalachian Mountains, the Rockies, along with other ranges of peaks that perhaps were not as lofty but equally beautiful in their own way. Whenever I saw them, the verse from the Psalms in the King James Version would come to my mind: "I will lift up mine eyes unto the mountains from whence cometh my help" (Psalm 121:1).

Keep On Moving?

We had started our Western jaunt by taking a northerly route, stopping to see Mammoth Cave in Kentucky, and then proceeding through Indianapolis and to Chicago, where a friend invited us to stay in his beautiful apartment on Lake Shore Drive. We were able to see a lot of the city, including going up in the Sears Tower, the tallest building in the U.S.A., and riding buses and the train.

When we went to the American Girl Place in suburban Chicago, where the popular collectible dolls are manufactured, Bonny Jean and Suzannah were delighted. We couldn't say the same, however, for the boys — for some reason, this toy mecca didn't seem to have the same appeal for them as the ESPN Zone Restaurant in New York City, for example. (Maybe if one of the American Girl dolls had been wearing a basketball uniform, the boys would have been a little more interested.)

Since David had meetings scheduled in Brookings, South Dakota, we decided to drive through North Dakota, so we could officially check that state off our list even though he didn't have any official business there. People had told us there was not much to see in Fargo, North Dakota, but a beautiful sunset we saw reflected in the snow was reason enough to justify that little "detour."

While we were in South Dakota, we elected to take some time to get off the beaten path and visit the historic Wall Drug Store. In planning our trip, we had agreed that we would include as many of the typical tourist stops as possible, but I felt it would be fun — and educational — for the children also to have the chance to visit some interesting places that were outside the normal tourism experience. The Wall Drug Store was one of our nontypical destinations.

I had read a magazine article about the drug store and thought it would be fascinating place for us to see. During World War II, it had seen a drastic decline in customers, so they decided to give away free ice water. They put up signs all over the region, "Stop at Wall Drugs for Free Ice Water." Ice water may no longer be its main attraction, but this quaint old drug store has become quite a tourist attraction, hearkening back to the days of the "general store" — perhaps the miniature forerunner of the discount superstores.

Driving on Water (The Frozen Kind)

In the South, the weather rarely stays cold enough to freeze surfaces of lakes to the point where you can safely stand on them. So it was an unusual experience for us to watch ice fishing in Minnesota. I had always preached to our children about never trying to walk on the ice if it covered the lake on our property, but we not only got to walk out on a lake in Minnesota, we also got to drive our RV onto it. In fact, just so he could say that he had done it, we let twelve-year-old Craig be the driver as we ventured out on the thick, frozen surface.

In Bloomington, Minnesota, a suburb of Minneapolis, we had a very different experience. We were given hotel accommodations from the company with which David was meeting, and the hotel was located across from the huge Mall of America, the largest, fully enclosed mall in the United States with more than 530 stores, over 50 restaurants, and many movie theaters and other entertainment centers. A brochure told us seven Yankee Stadiums could fit inside the mall, and another unique feature is that it houses an indoor amusement park which includes a roller coaster and a carousel. Our children received tickets for unlimited rides in the mall, and they took full advantage of that, after which we enjoyed touring an aquarium in the mall as a family.

I enjoyed our journey through the northern states, but as I have shared I would breathe a sigh of relief every time we passed through one of them because we had avoided getting caught in any major snowstorms. Since David had quite a few meetings arranged in the northern Midwest, the Weather Channel became one of our good friends during our time there. We certainly must have been an unusual sight for longtime residents of that region — an RV pulling a bicycle trailer, especially in temperatures with a wind chill as low as 14 degrees below zero.

Really Big on "Big Sky Country"

Craig, who turned thirteen during our trip, showed his love for the outdoors and natural beauty when I asked him what his favorites were on our trip. Shell Canyon in Wyoming was very special to him. In fact, he has already announced that when it comes time for him to go to college, he wants to go to the University of Wyoming in Laramie.

Other highlights, he said, included taking a plane ride over the glaciers in Alaska, which were "quite beautiful," Craig recalls, and spending several days at Lost Valley Ranch, a guest ranch in Sedalia, Colorado (near Colorado Springs). Set in a beautiful valley filled with pine trees and the grandeur of the Rocky Mountains, Lost Valley Ranch gave all of us a taste of cowboy living. We rode horses in the mountains through the snow, enjoyed seeing the cool mountain streams, and took part in a western-style cookout around a campfire.

After our time at the ranch, we proceeded to Breckenridge, Colorado, where we all had a great time snow skiing. I think if the children had more opportunities to ski, it would quickly become their sport of choice, although I don't know if the boys would ever let it usurp their love for team sports. We did try to emphasize to them that skiing is an expensive pastime, so it's not something that most people can afford to do very often.

While we were staying in Colorado Springs, heading off for a day of skiing, a good friend from home, Donelle Oldenburg Proctor, came to visit us. The kids were so thrilled to see a familiar face that they practically stumbled over each other so they could share with her about their personal travel adventures.

Fog, Fog, Go Away...

In March of 2001, we were in Arizona and looked forward to going to the Grand Canyon. Only David and I had seen it personally, but the rest of the family had seen photographs of it. I assured them that the photos can't begin to capture the visual impact of the canyon, so we were all excited about seeing it firsthand. We had stayed at a campground in the valley nearby, but as we drove to Grand Canyon National Park, the fog was so thick we could barely see the cars in front of us.

It was the only day we would be able to visit the park, so we all were disappointed by the likelihood of having come all this way and not be able to experience the fabled canyon in all of its grandeur. Some friends, Chuck and Melissa Tinney and four of their five children, had joined us for several days at this stage of the trip, so it looked like four adults and eight youngsters were in for a tremendous letdown.

The children suggested, "Why don't we pray about it?" asking God to lift the fog so we could enjoy seeing the Grand Canyon. So we did and then proceeded to purchase our tickets to enter the national park, even though the man at the ticket booth was skeptical that we would be able to see much. When David asked if the canyon was expected to be fogged in for the entire day, all he could tell us was, "I don't know. It looks like it might be."

Nevertheless, we drove into the park and hoped for the best. As we started to drive in, we couldn't see a thing. Simply believing the Grand Canyon was actually there was a real matter of faith. But then God did answer our prayers, no doubt, because the fog lifted totally and rolled away! In a very short time, we were overwhelmed by the most spectacular view of the canyon. From that time until sunset, we were enthralled by the ever-changing vistas of the canyon, seeing the play of colors as the sun moved to different parts of the sky.

There are many other examples of such instances during our travels, when we experienced the Lord hearing and responding to the simple prayers of a child. How exciting that was, not only to see God answer, but how our children prayed in such simple, trusting faith.

The day before we went to the Grand Canyon, David, and the boys had set off on a hike into the mountains. They were gone a long time, and Melissa and I began to grow concerned. We knew the trails they were following were snowy and icy, and while they had promised that they would be careful, we had heard stories about people slipping and sliding off mountainsides.

Finally, we saw David and the boys trudging back toward our RV. When David arrived, he announced that their trek "was not a mother trip — definitely a dad trip, not something a mom would let her child do." We didn't probe too much to find out exactly what exploits our beloved boys had done, all in the name of fun and masculinity. Sometimes, ignorance truly is bliss.

"Totally Cool" in New Mexico

Santa Fe, New Mexico, offered us yet another perspective of Americana. While we were there, we immersed ourselves in the Indian culture and drove to Bandoleer, where we saw the centuries-old cliff dwellings. We even got to climb the ladders and peer into the dwellings. Our climber, Scott, thought that was "totally cool." (Any time we went to a new place, he was quick to find something to climb, whether it was a rock wall, a tree, or some other obstacle that seemed to be calling out to him, "Climb me!")

Scott, who marked his twelfth birthday during our journey, displayed signs of becoming a rugged outdoorsman, just like his slightly older brother. He really took to the snowboarding and dogsledding in Alaska. However, one of his other favorites was a real contrast from that — San Antonio, Texas, and its famous Riverwalk.

The children found San Antonio a city that they really enjoyed, even asking to visit the Alamo twice. I can remember watching Walt Disney's Davy Crockett stories on TV when I was a little girl and learning about the Alamo. For some reason, I had always envisioned it as a huge fortress, but when we got there, we discovered it wasn't a lot bigger than a large house. No wonder Mexico's Santa Anna prevailed in the legendary battle!

We stayed in a hotel near the city's famed Riverwalk and enjoyed seeing some of the shops, as well as watching the people and seeing the tour boats move leisurely down the course of the river. This was another time when we were fortunate to "upgrade" to a better hotel room, actually being given the presidential suite at the Riverwalk Plaza Hotel. The balcony of our room overlooked the Riverwalk, which features a long, winding sidewalk and numerous shops along both sides of the San Antonio River, and we could see people casually strolling down the banks of the river. Since I love practical jokes, I let the children pour water off the balcony on unsuspecting pedestrians. This brought back memories of college days when I had done the same thing in San Antonio!

The Scent of A Sea Lion

During our westward swing, we visited the largest sea cave in the world, located near Florence, Oregon. To get to the cave, we descended more than two hundred feet in an elevator. The deeper we went, the stronger the smell of sea creatures became. By the time we reached the bottom and the door opened for us to step out, we were wishing for some clothespins to hold our noses.

We discovered the sea cave was full of sea lions — dark, hairy, "fragrant" sea lions. It was fun seeing them, but not smelling them. I don't guess anyone manufactures deodorant for sea lions. If you ever see a perfume called "Eau de Sea Lion," don't buy it! For the operators of the sea cave, the advantage of this overwhelming scent is probably that tourists won't want to stay for extended lengths of time, so the wait to get into the cave is never very long.

Going Camping — At Wal-Mart!

During our trip, our overnights were divided between nice campgrounds where we parked next to other highway nomads and, when it seemed more practical, to find a "room at the inn." But during our trip I had made an intriguing discovery — nearly one-third of RV travelers stay in Wal-Mart parking lots since they are very camper-friendly. I mentioned this to the children and you would have thought this was the greatest idea since Christmas. They were all for setting up at Wal-Mart for the night. You know how toddlers often have as much fun — or more — with a box than they do with the actual toy? I guess it was the same principle in action that our kids thought staying in a Wal-Mart parking lot would be far more fun than finding a suitable motel or campground. Their only question was, where would we find this Wal-Mart and how soon?

As it turned out, we decided to do this the night after we had been to the sea cave, following our drive north to the Seattle, Washington, area. The kids were more excited about that than going to Yosemite National Park. I understand there is a novel called *Where the Heart Is* about a troubled young woman who takes up residence in a Wal-Mart for a time. Well, we didn't move in; we just took advantage of the parking lot. It didn't matter — the children thought it was just great. They wanted us to select one that is open twenty-four hours so we could spend a little time strolling the aisles whenever we wanted.

Instead, we found an "old-fashioned" Wal-Mart that was not open around the clock, but the children still thought it was neat to be there to close the store down for the night. My opinion? Well, I'm glad that we had the experience, but I don't think it's one that we really need to repeat. From my perspective, I would say that if you have camped at one Wal-Mart, you have camped at them all.

In the backs of our minds, we wondered if we had brought with us any of the residue from our visit with the sea lions, but no one said anything. If they had been available, we would have been glad to take showers. Perhaps the Wal-Marts should consider making such facilities available, at least in sea lion country.

Calling All Park Rangers

Throughout our trip, we seemed to be magnets for park rangers. This was due, in part, because many of the campgrounds we stayed in were located in state and national parks. But it was also because with our curiosity and spirit of adventure, we sometimes found ourselves in places where even park rangers fear to tread.

There was the time we were driving from Arizona to Zion Canyon in Utah, which seemed like a good shortcut to Las Vegas, Nevada, one of the cities where David had meetings scheduled. It was very late at night as we neared the canyon, driving up a winding mountain road. When we had nearly reached the point where we expected to find the canyon, we saw a roadside sign that read, "Oversized vehicles cannot use the tunnel to go through to the canyon without an escort from the park rangers." *Now they tell us, we thought.*

The sign also stated that vehicles could go through the tunnel — which had been cut through a mountain — only between certain hours, and we were already well past that time. Because of the narrow road, we knew it would be difficult to turn around, especially in the dark. We wondered, "Are we going to be stuck here? What are we going to do?"

David decided to call a special number that we saw posted on one of the signs. The ranger who answered stated he was not supposed to allow anyone into the canyon that late at night, but if we could get to the entrance of the tunnel within fifteen minutes, he would meet us there to guide us through. As promised, the ranger was there when we arrived and directed us to drive down the center line of the tunnel, since he was concerned that with the size of our RV, we might scrape against the tunnel walls or even get hung up somewhere.

As we exited the tunnel, we could imagine the beauty all around us but could not see much because of the darkness. But when we stopped at one of the pull-off areas and got out to walk around, we saw the moon appearing gigantic in the horizon. As we gazed into the distance, we could see the moonlight jumping off the canyon walls, creating an absolutely fabulous display of light and shadow. We couldn't imagine a prettier evening.

One day in New Mexico, we were surprised to find a volcano; we decided to drive up the side of it in the RV, trying to ignore the steep drop-off on the other side of the road. There was some snow and ice on the road, so we were very cautious as we drove up. Finally, we reached the top of the volcano and got out of the motor home, glad for the chance to stretch out and experience being perched atop a volcano, even though it was inactive.

We were having a good time — but we frankly were dreading the drive back down the volcano. Suddenly, a park ranger came up to us and asked, "What are you all doing here? Didn't you read the sign that said you're not supposed to be up here? Especially in an RV pulling a trailer!" Honestly, we hadn't seen that sign, but we were grateful to have an experienced park ranger to lead the way back down.

Once we reached the bottom, we could understand why we shouldn't have been up there. We made it down without any trouble, but it had been a frightening descent. Remember the old saying about fools rushing in where angels fear to tread? During our travels, there were times I'm sure we kept park rangers — and angels — working overtime.

ARE WE GOING TO THE MOUNTAIN WITH THE HEADS IN IT?

Skiing in Breckenridge, Colorado

Beautiful Pass in Washington State

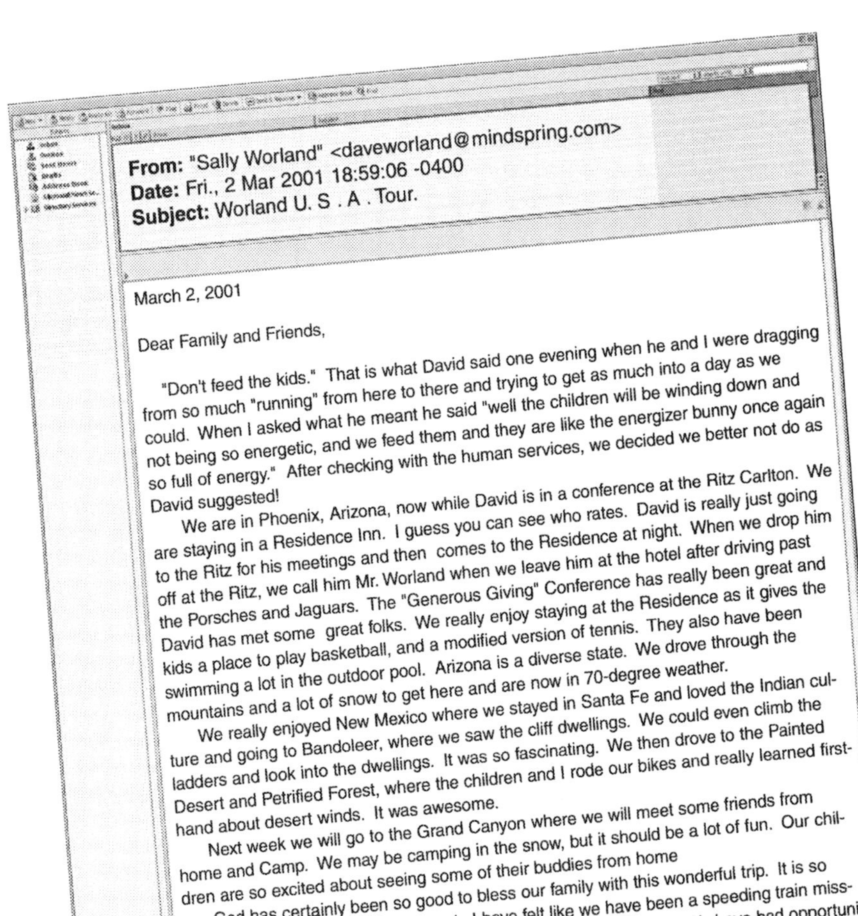

From: "Sally Worland" <daveworland@mindspring.com>
Date: Fri., 2 Mar 2001 18:59:06 -0400
Subject: Worland U. S . A . Tour.

March 2, 2001

Dear Family and Friends,

"Don't feed the kids." That is what David said one evening when he and I were dragging from so much "running" from here to there and trying to get as much into a day as we could. When I asked what he meant he said "well the children will be winding down and not being so energetic, and we feed them and they are like the energizer bunny once again so full of energy." After checking with the human services, we decided we better not do as David suggested!

We are in Phoenix, Arizona, now while David is in a conference at the Ritz Carlton. We are staying in a Residence Inn. I guess you can see who rates. David is really just going to the Ritz for his meetings and then comes to the Residence at night. When we drop him off at the Ritz, we call him Mr. Worland when we leave him at the hotel after driving past the Porsches and Jaguars. The "Generous Giving" Conference has really been great and David has met some great folks. We really enjoy staying at the Residence as it gives the kids a place to play basketball, and a modified version of tennis. They also have been swimming a lot in the outdoor pool. Arizona is a diverse state. We drove through the mountains and a lot of snow to get here and are now in 70-degree weather.

We really enjoyed New Mexico where we stayed in Santa Fe and loved the Indian culture and going to Bandoleer, where we saw the cliff dwellings. We could even climb the ladders and look into the dwellings. It was so fascinating. We then drove to the Painted Desert and Petrified Forest, where the children and I rode our bikes and really learned first-hand about desert winds. It was awesome.

Next week we will go to the Grand Canyon where we will meet some friends from home and Camp. We may be camping in the snow, but it should be a lot of fun. Our children are so excited about seeing some of their buddies from home

God has certainly been so good to bless our family with this wonderful trip. It is so neat to see His hand in every aspect. I have felt like we have been a speeding train missing the bad weather by a day or even a few hours in many places. We have had opportunities to meet so many nice people and to feel a part of their life for a short time.

Please keep your e-mails coming as we love to hear stories from home. May God bless and keep you.

Love,
Sally, David, Craig, Scott, Bonny Jean, and Suzannah.

CHAPTER SIX

And Then We Were Six

The Worland family's trans-United States saga would be incomplete without telling how we became a family of six in the first place. That by itself is a story of considerable complexity.

Our first three children arrived very closely together, over a span of a little more than three years. Craig came first on August 31, 1987, followed by Scott on October 11, 1988, and finally, Bonny Jean on January 29, 1991. After being blessed by three wonderful youngsters, David and I felt it would be an incredible experience to adopt a child to round out our family.

We actually first talked about adopting children before we got married. We started discussing and praying about this possibility again in 1994, and this idea became stronger when we were guests at a conference on charitable giving that was being held in Cancun, Mexico, in October 1995. The event had attracted philanthropists and representatives from a variety of charitable organizations. The accommodations were outstanding, and we felt fortunate to be surrounded by people who were strongly committed to supporting charitable causes.

The upscale hotel that served as the setting for the conference, however, was a stark contrast to what we witnessed not far from the hotel. As we walked around Cancun, we saw a side of the city that travel agencies don't illustrate in their vacation brochures. We observed people living in extreme poverty, like nothing David had ever witnessed before, and I had only seen while on short-term missions trips to Haiti and North Africa. There were so many children barely surviving, seemingly without even the most basic of necessities.

Seeing these helpless ones stirred our hearts. There was such a great need, and although we knew we could not help all of these children, we realized that if the Lord was willing, we could provide a home for at least one. Perhaps, we thought, we should investigate how to go about adopting.

When we returned to the hotel, I overhead a woman telling someone, "I'm in charge of adoptions in Ukraine." There were many needy children in Cancun, but I knew there were hundreds of children also desperately in need of homes in counties like the Ukraine and other parts of the former Soviet Union and Eastern Europe.

Even before the conference I had been thinking a lot about adopting a child from another part of the world. Seeing the destitute Mexican children and hearing the woman who coordinated Ukranian adoptions peaked my interest even more, so I approached David about it when we got back to our room. Being aware of how costly adoptions are, he responded in a very practical way: "Well, let's pray about it for a couple of months."

I knew David meant what he said and wasn't just trying to put me off, but in my impatience I responded, "I *have* been praying about it for a long time, and I want some action." My husband, being the wonderful man that he is, simply looked at me and said, "Let's just pray about it."

And pray about it we did! While I did a little research, I discovered that for several reasons, including the fact that we already had three children, agencies that coordinated adoptions in Mexico, Vietnam, and China would not consider us. However, adoptions from Eastern European nations did not carry the same restrictions. It did not matter to us where the child came from; the main stipulation would be that the child be a girl and younger than Bonny Jean, so we could keep our children's birth order the same.

I came home one December evening from shopping and found David sitting at a table in our kitchen, filling out a massive pile of forms. They were applications to start the adoption process. True to his word, he had been praying about it for two months and it was time, he had decided, "for action." He told me the only reason he had not joined with me in pursuing adoption earlier was the cost; he had determined that he would simply trust God with that and get things started.

We learned the total cost for adopting a child would exceed $20,000, which caused us to take a huge gulp together. We had only about $2,000 saved that we could use as a down payment — earnest money, you might say — but had no idea from where the rest would come. All we knew for certain was that God had given us a desire to adopt a child and we were only being obedient in doing our part. He would have to do the rest.

As it turned out, the "simple" matter of giving a home to a child from another land took us two-and-a-half years and included several great disappointments. There was a little girl from Latvia that we were supposed to adopt. We had received a lot of information about Christina and photographs of her, and we had even decided that we would give her the name Maria.

Then we received a telephone call informing us that she had been adopted through another agency and would be living in Texas. We never got a full explanation of how that mix-up occurred, but regardless, it was heartbreaking after all the anticipation that the children and we had felt as the adoption day had drawn closer.

After picking our hearts up off the floor, we decided to try again. This time the plan was for us to adopt two little sisters — the agency understandably did not want the siblings to be separated. Our intention had been to adopt only one child, feeling we could not afford more than that and really did not have enough space in our home, but we wanted to be open to however God would lead. If He wanted us to add two to our family, we knew He certainly would provide whatever we needed to make that possible.

As is my practice when I'm facing a difficult decision or troublesome issue, I took a walk to clear my head and try to discern what we should do. I can still vividly remember the grandeur of that fall day — the crisp temperature, the bright blue sky, the beautiful trees and little animals scurrying around. I sat down on a rock and said aloud, "I don't know if I can do this!"

At that moment, I felt a soft and steady breeze rubbing against my cheek. I can't explain it, but it seemed as if God were saying to me, "If I can take care of all the children in the world, don't you think I can help you take care of two more children in your family?" How could I say no to that? I returned home with a renewed sense that this is what we should do — and when I told David, he simply said, "Go for it!" and I called the agency to tell them we wanted to proceed.

Having adjusted our thinking to seeing our family expand from five to seven, David and I busily prepared to travel to Latvia to pick up the girls. We were just days away from leaving when again we received a phone call. This time the adoption agency informed us that the girls, whose Russian names were Ekatarina and Ludmila, had gone to live with their grandparents.

Although we were pleased to hear that they were going to be with close family members, we still felt heartsick that these little girls whom we had already grown to love through their photos and the information the agency had provided about them would not become part of our family after all. Although the adoption had never become official, we still felt that in a way, they had been snatched from us. It really seemed like losing members of our own family.

Finally, losing patience with the process and tiring of the emotional roller coaster we were riding, David and I decided to travel to Russia and try to expedite the process of adopting yet another child — also named Christina — who had been offered to us through Russian officials. The U.S.-based agency with which we were working with had advised us that being there in person might help. So we embarked on a twenty-seven hour journey to Kalingrad, Russia, traveling more than 13,000 miles on three planes, hopeful that at last we would find the little girl the Lord wanted us to adopt.

Much to our dismay, we discovered Christina's information had been falsified. We found that she was a four-year-old girl who was profoundly disabled. She could not speak clearly and probably would never be able to do so. The director of the orphanage said the little girl most likely would never have a mentality beyond that of a two-year-old, and we saw numerous bite marks where she had bitten herself.

Having traveled so far to encounter yet another setback, we felt very confused. With our family situation, having three children already, we were expecting to find a child who was relatively healthy. We had not prepared ourselves, emotionally or in any other way, for a child who would require a great commitment of time, money, and specialized care. However, once again we resorted to prayer, which had sustained us so often: "Lord, if you brought us here to bring this little girl home, and if You're telling us this is what You want us to do, then we want to do what You want." Experience in working with disabled people for twenty-five years at Recreation Ranch, a therapeutic horsemanship program I co-founded with a longtime friend, Donelle Oldenburg Proctor, I understood the needs of the disabled. I wanted to have an open heart to what God had in mind for us.

As it turned out, we were informed that the little girl was not yet adoptable anyway, that the bureaucratic red tape was still far from complete and would remain so for quite some time. Learning this gave us a great sense of peace, even though we didn't know what our next steps should be in trying to finalize an adoption. It seemed as if God were saying to us, "Just wait on me. I will provide the right child at the right time."

Since we were already in Kalingrad, we resolved to search every orphanage we could find and see if there might be a child somewhere waiting for us. After we had been there for four days, we were told one afternoon that there was a child available at a particular orphanage, but we had to get there before 5 o'clock. So our driver, Vladmir, rushed us over there, bouncing the tiny car across narrow roads rutted with potholes and pressing us from one side of the vehicle to the other as he careened around tight corners. Obviously not designed for comfort, the car had no seatbelts and our heads frequently bounced against the ceiling of the car.

It was not that Vladmir was a bad driver; he simply understood the urgency of getting us there before the deadline. His efforts paid off as he got us there just minutes before five. Quickly, we were introduced to the little girl, whose name was Julia. David and I agreed, "All right, we'll take this child," and went to the consulate in the city, presuming we could finalize the arrangements.

But we had another disappointment in store for us. The atmosphere at the consulate was cold and unyielding; for some reason it made me think that this must have been what it felt like during the recently ended Communist reign. The woman we approached there about adopting Julia barely gave us a hearing. There was no way she was going to let us take her to the United States.

Our time had run out, and we needed to board the airplane for the first segment of our trip back home. After all we had gone through, we were returning with empty arms and heavy hearts. We could not understand why we had run into so many roadblocks. We had told God we were open to whatever plan He had for expanding our family, but to that point we had experienced no success at all.

Despite one disappointment after another, we could not let go of the idea of adopting a little girl. We knew that around the world there were so many children in desperate need of good homes, and we wanted to open ours up to one of them. Equally important, we knew what a special blessing it would be for our family and for Bonny Jean to have a little sister. David called me an eternal optimist because I was convinced that God still had a special child reserved just for us. The Bible speaks often about the virtues of perseverance, and we certainly were well on the path to become virtuous, at least in that area.

In the summer of 1997, we had an opportunity to meet with Peggy Lowe, a staff member in the Chattanooga office of Bethany Christian Services, which is based in Michigan. She had done our original home study for the adoption agency, since they did not have a representative in our area. We explained to Peggy about our situation and how our efforts to adopt a little girl had been frustrated again and again. Bethany has provided adoption services in the United States and around the world for many years, and she told us the Chattanooga office had just started working in the area of international adoptions. She asked if she could pray with us and see if God might want us to try to find a child through Bethany.

We knew that to switch agencies at this point would be costly, because we basically would have to start over. This would entail reapplying for immigration papers, since the documents we had were expiring, along with new doctor's physicals, being fingerprinted again (this time at an attorney's office, rather than the Walker County Sheriff's office), and other necessary details that are part of the adoption process. But after having explored every avenue for about two years with our present agency without success, we thought this might be the course we should take. We would be the first family to pursue an international adoption through Bethany's Chattanooga office. Once again we filled out the extensive paperwork, went through Bethany's screening process, fulfilled all the other requirements, and then. . . waited.

In September, we received a call from Peggy. She excitedly told us about a little four-year-old girl in Krasnodar, Russia, that they wanted us to consider. Unlike the other children we had expected to adopt, however, the only things we knew about this child was that her Russian name was Valentina, and that she was supposed to be healthy.

Aware that we might be getting on yet another emotional roller coaster, we told Peggy we were ready to move ahead. Bethany sent us videos of the little girl and, once more, we began to love a child in a distant land as we had the others. Admittedly, our feelings were somewhat more reserved than before since we didn't want to endure heartbreak again.

We tried to take a step back, believing it wasn't fair to our young children to allow them to become too attached to another little girl they anticipated would become their sister. This time, we didn't put her photos all around our house or spend time viewing her video repeatedly. We simply determined that if Valentina were the child God had planned for us, He would work it all out.

Late in 1997, the Bethany office called and assured us the adoption would be going through. Initially, we were scheduled to go to Russia in December to get her, but we ran into another delay in getting documents processed, so our trip was postponed until January 1998. Having to wait was hard, because our excitement was growing and we hoped that our family would finally become six. We had decided to rename her Suzannah Sally, giving her my name as a middle name, following a practice we had established of naming our children after members of my family. (David said since all the children would have his last name, he thought it would be nice to select their middle names from my side of the family.)

On January 26, 1998, David and I boarded our first flight in Chattanooga, changing planes in Atlanta and proceeding to Moscow. The final leg of our trip was from Moscow to

Krasnodar on a domestic Russian airline. It was a case of boarding an airplane and wondering, "Who built this?" If someone had told me the plane was held together with bailing wire, I would have believed it. I expected Candid Camera to pop out anytime.

When I sat on my seat, the seat back fell backward. My seatbelt also would not work, and the racks where everyone stored their luggage had no doors, so luggage would slide back and forth. Several times we thought bags were about to fall on our heads. David, who was seated across the aisle from me, and I looked at each other and said, "Well, the Lord brought us here — and we're sure He is going to take care of us." Just to be sure, I kept reminding Him that I had three other children back home who really needed me!

Arriving in Krasnodar, we were met by Olga, a loving and self-sacrificing woman, who was to serve as our facilitator and translator. We learned that she was a professor with a doctorate in English in American Southern literature, and when she learned that we were from the Southeastern United States, it led to a very enjoyable conversation on the way to the house where we would spend the night before going to the orphanage the next morning.

Our hosts that night were a couple named Sasha and Valya. They had a very humble home with only the barest of essentials, and even though they had eight children, they freely shared their home with us. What a gesture of love and selflessness that was!

Since we could hardly contain our excitement, David and I barely slept at all that night. When morning arrived, Olga drove us from the city to the rural area of Otradnaya, about a five-hour drive outside of Krasnodar, where the orphanage was located. We entered the property through a gate and were encouraged by seeing that the grounds were well — attended, even though there was nothing ostentatious about the setting.

When we were introduced to the director of the orphanage, she smiled and said, Momma, your new daughter looks like you!" We had not yet met the little girl, so that surprised me because we had not seen a resemblance in photos of her that we had received. Soon, we heard outside the door of the director's office the sound of several women fussing over "Suzannah." Finally, the door opened and the wonderful little girl walked in and declared, "Momma, I love you!" and gave me a great big hug. She was wearing a huge red bow that covered hair that was very thin, we later learned, because of years of poor nutrition. The people at the orphanage had done their best to make Suzannah look presentable, but I noticed that her dress looked and smelled soiled.

The director looked at us and asked if we wanted this child. As if we were going to say that we didn't want a child that had just said that she loved us. The fact is, we already loved her and considered her one of our own.

With Suzannah in tow, the director gave us a tour of the orphanage. The experience of seeing dozens of other little children, also in need of loving homes, was overwhelming. We felt a sense of helplessness, but this was tempered by our joy in knowing that we were now going to be bringing one special child into our family.

In addition, we had brought a huge duffle bag bulging with gifts from friends and members in our Sunday school class for us to give to the other children at the orphanage. We showed them first to Suzannah and then asked her to help us in distributing them to the other children. It was so interesting to see the changing expressions on her face: First, she was elated to see all the special clothes and toys we had brought, items she had never seen before, let alone possess. Then she reflected a mixture of delight and regret in presenting them to the children she would be leaving behind. Deep down, however, I think she realized it was one final gesture of kindness she could provide, knowing she was going on to a loving home while they would be remaining in the orphanage.

Next we returned to the director's office, where we met with several other people, including social workers. Suzannah stayed with us the entire time — I was not about to let her out of my sight now that we finally had her. We were told the story of her past, which we had not yet heard.

Local family welfare representatives had found the little girl, named Valentina, when she was about three years old. Unbelievably, although she was little more than a baby herself, she was caring for her eighteen-month-old baby half-brother, Alex. Her "house" was merely a tiny hut with a dirt floor. It had no beds, or bed clothes, running water, electricity, and neither she nor her brother was wearing a stitch of clothing. The filth in their little home was terrible beyond description. (And interestingly, the official documents commented that Valentina "had no place to dream.")

Authorities managed to find their mother, who was a troubled young woman who had to resort to desperate means to make money and had turned to alcohol to ease her painful existence. After making several unsuccessful attempts to reconcile the mother to her children, the officials took them away. Before they could be taken to a children's home, however, the children had to be admitted to a hospital for treatment of respiratory and skin problems they had developed in their horrific living conditions.

A short time later, a Russian family adopted the brother directly from the hospital, but Valentina had to remain in the hospital for another three months while she was being treated for a variety of ailments, including rickets, which results from a severe calcium deficiency. Finally, she was taken to the orphanage, about a year and a half before we found her.

To this day, Suzannah can remember how much she loved it when it snowed because she could eat the snow for water. Although such a young age, she instinctively knew she had to do whatever it took to survive, including eating anything she could find that was edible — even insects.

After hearing this story, Olga admitted in amazement that if she had known what a difficult life Suzannah had already experienced, she would not have recommended her for adoption, being fearful of many problems that could arise due to her background. We could understand her concern, but even though we had known Suzannah only a few hours, we were so glad that God didn't have such reservations.

Before we left the orphange, we had to remove every stitch of her clothing and replace it with clothes we had brought with us from America. The soiled dress Suzannah was wearing, we were informed, was the same dress every little girl — regardless of size — wore when she was presented to prospective adoptive parents.

Suzannah, who as it turns out does look like me, became a member of our family in January 1998, although her official adoption date is December 25, 1997. Evidently, the paperwork for the adoption was completed in Russia on Christmas Day, meaning God was preparing a very special Christmas present for us that we didn't even know we had at the time.

I cannot express the excitement, joy, and relief David and I felt when the process finally had been completed. After encountering one delay after another, and having to overcome great disappointments, we could hardly believe that Suzannnah was our very own. I hope the other children we had thought we would be adopting all are happy in their new homes, but we are so thankful the Lord had us wait until He led us to her.

From the time we began trying to adopt a child, especially after the first disappointments, I often said that I would believe the little girl we adopted was truly ours when she was asleep in her own bed in our home. I still have a photograph of Suzannah, asleep in her bed, that first night that she was officially home with us.

Ultimately, we spent more than $33,000 to adopt Suzannah, including the three instances when we lost children that we had been expected to be able to adopt, and starting over again when we changed adoption agencies.

Throughout the process, we frequently prayed, "God, if you want us to adopt a child, You will provide a way." And He did supply the resources to cover the costs, often in what we would consider miraculous ways. One time, for example, we received an anonymous donation of $5,000 to help with our expenses. To this day, we have no idea who the donor was, but the money came at an ideal time since we were preparing for our trip to Kalingrad. We never had mentioned any financial need, but we also received many other unsolicited and anonymous donations to assist us. We will forever be tremendously grateful and thankful for each of these generous friends and their gifts.

There were times, however , when it became necessary to put substantial expenses on our credit cards. Suzannah was the first and only child we ever had to put on a credit card! I was really glad when we were finally able to pay off those bills, because we didn't want her to be collateral for our debts!

Her past is becoming a fading memory, but remnants remain that still influence her behavior at times. Before we left Russia to bring Suzannah home to the United States, we stayed at a hotel in Moscow and inadvertently ordered sushi. David and I don't like sushi, but Suzannah grabbed it with gusto and ate piece after piece of the uniquely prepared raw fish. We had been advised just to let her eat whatever she wanted, because that would be better than trying to make her stop. As she virtually inhaled the sushi, we marveled, thinking about the inner strength God had given so she could survive her first years that had been so tragic and destitute. Before we left Russia, we even gave Suzannah her first haircut. She had so little hair and many bald spots from the poor nutrition that it was difficult to style her hair.

We know nothing about her little brother, but the tender care that she gave him is still a part of her today. Suzannah is a true caregiver, someone whose concern and energy for others is boundless.

One Sunday, while we were in Alaska during our trip across the United States, we realized that geographically she was closer to her old homeland in Russia than she was to our home in Georgia. Emotionally, however, Suzannah was farther away from her homeland than ever; it was amazing to realize how wonderfully she had fit into our family — it seemed almost as if she had been a part of us from the beginning.

Officially, she is closer to the U.S.A. than Russia as well. Almost immediately after bringing Suzannah home, we completed the massive amounts of paperwork to apply for her American citizenship, and on May 11, 1999, our entire family — including my parents — drove to Atlanta, Georgia, where she was sworn in as a U.S. citizen. Often, when people ask what was involved in obtaining citizenship for Suzannah, I tell them she had to learn the Bill of Rights and the Constitution, and memorize the names of all the presidents and their wives. (And if they believe that, I make up some more "requirements" until they realize that I'm teasing them about what is expected of a six-year-old.)

Near the end of our fifty-state trip, we celebrated Mother's Day on May 12, 2001, in Oahu, Hawaii. We began the day by going to a worship service at a church nearby. The message that morning fit beautifully not only with our own travels but also with the personal pilgrimage Suzannah had made since January, 1998. The pastor of the church gave a sermon from Romans 8 that states we become adopted as children of God when we commit our lives to Jesus Christ. I'll never forget the sweet look of wonder on Suzannah's face when she turned to me and said, "Mommie, I've been adopted two times!"

Suzannah has become such a light in the life of our family and brings us much joy, along with Bonny Jean, whom she admires so much, and her brothers, Craig and Scott, who are so devoted to her. We can see now that all the delays and setbacks were simply God's way of directing us to Suzannah. Today, we can't imagine our family without her, and as you'll soon see, our trip across the United States would not have been the same either.

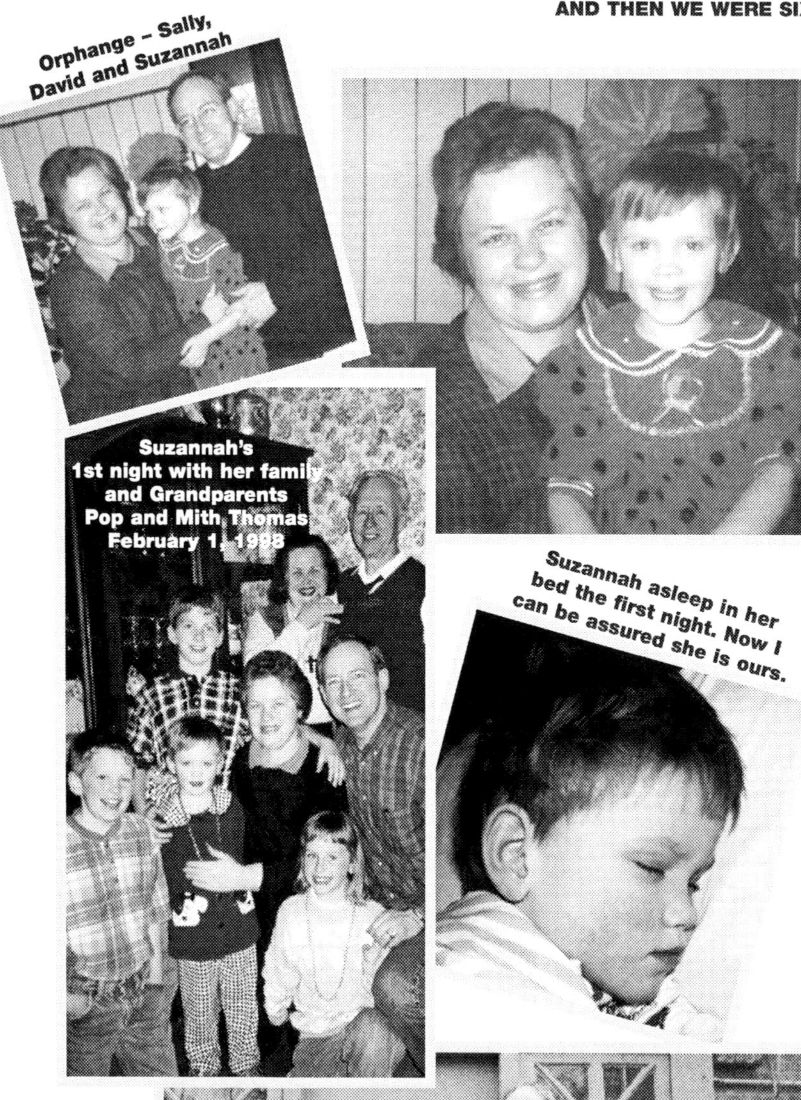

Orphange – Sally, David and Suzannah

Suzannah's 1st night with her family and Grandparents Pop and Mith Thomas February 1, 1998

Suzannah asleep in her bed the first night. Now I can be assured she is ours.

Oldga (our wonderful facilitator)

Krasnodar, Russia

Otradnaya Orphange

April 25, 1998

Dear Family and Friends

As we reflect on the Easter Season, we recall the incredible love our Lord has for us. He offered us eternal life by His death and resurrection. He also said:

" I am come that they might have life, and that they might have it more abundantly" John 10:10b. We are thankful for the abundant life God has given us with our family and friends.

On April 15th, 1993, one of God's children was born into this world in a small agricultural village of Otradnensky in southern Russia. The first three years of her life were spent in a one room, dirt floor hut. As the court papers read, "She had no place to dream." Which literally meant she had no bed, but accurately represented her life. With no family able to keep her, she was given medical treatment and placed in an orphanage.

On December 25th, 1997, A court in Krasnador, Russia approved us as the adoptive family for this precious four year old girl.

On January 27th, 1998, we were finally allowed to meet our daughter, pick her up and complete all the paperwork to bring her home. Everyone associated with Bethany Christian Services, that facilitated the adoption process, was wonderful.

On February 1st, 1998, we returned home and introduced Suzannah Sally Worland to her brothers and sister, Grandparents, Aunts and Uncles, and approximately sixty-five well-wishers from the church and community.

You are important to our family and we wanted to share this blessing with you. Our prayer is that God may richly bless you during this year. May the beauty of spring remind you of the continuing promises He fulfills.

"For as many as may be the promises of God, in Him they are yes: wherefore also by Him is our Amen to the glory of God through us." 2Cor1:20

"My daughter, shall I not seek security for you, that it may be well with you?"
Ruth 3:1B

In Christ's Love,
David, Sally, Craig, Scott, Bonny Jean, and Suzannah Worland

CHAPTER SEVEN

Family Escapades "Will We Have to Buy the Hotel?"

As you might expect, if you spend the better part of a year traveling and staying in unfamiliar surroundings, you can expect a lot of surprises — many of them pleasant, but some not so pleasant. For instance, there was the time we almost set fire to the hotel where we were staying for about a week.

It was a very nice hotel in Kansas City, Missouri — one of those where they give you a free chocolate cookie at the front desk when you check in. I have always thought that is such a nice gesture — especially since our boys can eat about a dozen in one sitting.

We had rented a suite to accommodate the children and me for eight days, since David had to catch a flight for a conference in Atlanta. It was too cold to stay at a local campground, and when he was away, David preferred that we book a room at a quality hotel or motel. The suite had many conveniences, including a refrigerator, coffeemaker, hair dryer, two TV sets — and even a microwave oven.

As I mentioned earlier, we had a microwave oven in the RV, but Suzannah thought it was especially neat to have one in our hotel room. The day after we arrived, she decided it would be nice to warm up her cookie so it would taste as if it were freshly baked. She set the microwave on 25 and then walked off to do something. Unfortunately, her 25 was for 25 minutes, not 25 seconds! (Don't try this at home.)

I was in another part of the suite and suddenly I smelled something hot. I rushed into the part of the suite where Suzannah had been and saw smoke billowing out of the microwave. The paper plate on which she had placed the cookie had gotten so hot that it caught fire, and the cookie had been burned to a crisp. Following its programmed instructions, the microwave continued to hum along, so I quickly turned it off. When I opened the door, more smoke poured out and filled our room, as well as the hallway outside of the suite!

I opened all the windows in our suite and began fanning the sprinkler system and smoke alarms in the room, fearful that at any moment our room would become flooded by torrents of water from the sprinkler system in the ceiling. Through the smoke and the haze in the hallway, I could see other guests of the hotel — some of them in their pajamas — wondering what was going on in the suite down the hall. Then I saw the manager hurriedly coming toward us. I explained what had happened and offered assurances to all of the onlookers that everything was okay, but I suspect that some people weren't too sure.

Fortunately, the sprinkler system did not activate, so the furnishings in our room and our personal belongings were spared. I wouldn't say that the children and I panicked, but we came reasonably close. At one point, while wrestling with my concern that if the sprinklers did come on they would cause widespread damage, a thought passed through my mind: *Will we have to buy the hotel?*

Thankfully, permanent damage was avoided, but the odor of the smoke from the charred cookie and paper plate lingered throughout our stay at the hotel. Despite this inconvenience, we all learned a valuable lesson: When you "nuke" a cookie in a microwave oven, make sure you're doing it only for seconds, not minutes!

Letting Kids Just Be Kids

I'm a firm believer in letting kids be kids and giving them an opportunity to just have fun. Certainly, they need to be respectful and demonstrate good manners, but it's also important to give them the freedom to let out their childhood exuberance. The old saying states that you're only a child once, but besides that, the time of being a child isn't very long at all, especially in terms of an entire lifetime. So, I'm a big advocate of allowing and encouraging our children to experience life as a child should, in a fun way.

For this reason, I might sometimes be guilty of letting the children do things that other adults would frown on. We were in Pigeon Forge, Tennessee, staying at a motel with an indoor water slide that was 100 feet long. Now that is a slide! The kids and I swam for a couple of hours and had a terrific time. During that time it occurred to me that perhaps there's still a lot of kid left in me, because I heard another mother reprimanding her children for doing something that I thought was just a case of kids having fun. They will have the rest of their lives to be adults—the clock is already ticking down on their childhood years, and I just don't want them to grow up too fast.

Part of being a child is indulging in a little mischievous activity — or just doing something silly as long as it doesn't hurt anybody. For instance, we were in Milwaukee, Wisconsin, in February 2001, staying at a hotel that also had an indoor swimming pool. This one did not have a 100-foot slide, but it was fun to be frolicking in the warm water and look outside the glass enclosure at the snow covering the ground on a 0° degree day.

We started playing a game of "Truth or Dare," in which the participants compete to catch each other making a false statement. If a person is caught telling something that is not true, he or she has to do some kind of silly stunt. As our game progressed that day, the dares got more challenging. Finally, we dared each other to run around the outside of the hotel through the snow and come back in through a back door into the pool area. Running through snow in a swimsuit in the dead of winter in Wisconsin wasn't exactly at the top of my "must-do" list, but I figured, what's the harm? Anyway, we were the only ones there — or so we thought.

One by one, the children responded to the dare and raced around the hotel, tramping through the snow and back to the pool. Then the children dared me to do it too, barefoot and clad only in my swimsuit. Not wanting to be outdone, I took off running. As I reentered by the back door, I found out we weren't the only ones there after all. First, I met a man who apparently was a guest at the hotel — and then I encountered David, who first looked shocked and then asked the obvious: "What in the world are you doing?" (I'm not sure that he ever let the other man know that we were his family.)

It wasn't planned this way, but not long afterward we were bound for Texas, where David had quite a few meetings scheduled. Before we knew it, we had gone from 10 degrees below zero to 60 degrees above zero. It was a tremendous temperature swing (we blamed that for the colds we all came down with about the same time), and after the "truth or dare" episode, I think David was glad to get us away from snow.

Polishing Up a Friendship

There was the time when we were in Kansas City, visiting in the home of a family who had lost a child in a swimming pool drowning accident several years earlier. We were having a wonderfully encouraging time with them, learning how God's grace had sustained them during that tragic circumstance, when we noticed that Suzannah and two of their daughters had been out of the room for quite a while. Then we noticed the strong odor of fingernail polish.

The three girls, we quickly discovered, had decided to exercise their artistic bent on each other, painting one another with the bright pink polish, with most of it going on the youngest daughter. We worked for more than an hour to get her cleaned up, using fingernail polish remover, cooking oil, and even Vaseline to try to take polish off her, but she still was wearing shiny pink spots when it was time for us to leave.

The family was very kind about the incident but it did put a damper on our visit, and we emphatically explained to Suzannah that fingernail polish is not at all the same as finger paint, but we just chalked up that event as a learning experience for all of us. Needless to say, Suzannah now understands that *fingernail* polish is just for fingernails, and even then, only when she is being supervised.

Our Friends, the Park Rangers

As I mentioned earlier, we developed a habit of finding ways to give park rangers a greater sense of job security. One instance occurred while we were staying at a campground on the San Diego Bay in California. David and the kids thought the idea of taking a swim in the bay would be great, so they headed for the water, not for a moment considering there could be anything wrong with that. Meanwhile, I jumped on my bicycle to ride to the camp store.

Along the way I noticed a sign by the boat dock that read, "No swimming. Contaminated water." After pondering that for a moment, I presumed they meant that the gasoline from the boats was the problem, so I didn't think much about it. But just to be safe, I decided to inquire about the sign when I got to the store. The store clerk very seriously warned me that the entire bay had become contaminated because of the runoff from a recent heavy rain, so I hopped back on my bike to warn David.

By the time I got to the shore along the bay, all I found were four empty bikes. "Uh, oh," I thought. After spending the next couple of minutes frantically searching for my family, I found David and the kids at the showers. They had actually gone into the bay and were happily swimming when a ranger came along and informed David that the water was contaminated, so he and the children needed to get out immediately. The ranger hustled them to the showers nearby, where David and children scrubbed like never before.

We never did find out why a sign was not posted at the swimming area to warn about the contaminated water. Maybe the park officials just felt a real live ranger would be more convincing than a stationary sign. If that was their thinking, they were absolutely right.

How Much for Half a Dozen Haircuts?

Another event we had not thought about much before we initially headed out on the American highway was how to handle the logistics of haircuts. I chuckle when I think of the first time we tried to find a hair shop for five haircuts. (I had decided to forgo getting a haircut that time.) The first place we stopped was asking $17.00

for each boy's haircut and up to $40.00 for an adult haircut — not exactly what we had factored into our budget! Seeing no need to mortgage our home back in Georgia just to get some heads of hair cut, we continued to hunt around for a better price. We went to five shops until we finally found one that would give us a package deal, five haircuts for $88.00. That was still costly, but compared to the first price we had received, it sounded like a bargain!

Worland, Wyoming — Our Kind of Town

I'm certain you recognize that *Worland* will never rival Smith, Johnson, or Jones as one of the most common last names in the United States. Outside of our immediate family, we have not encountered very many Worlands over the years. So, it was a very special highlight for each of us in April 2001 as our trip began winding down to spend a few days in Worland, Wyoming.

Have you ever visited a town or city named after your forefathers? David had known about the city of Worland for years, first hearing about it while he was still a boy at a family reunion in 1965. The Indiana branch of David's family had done a research project in the mid-'60s and traced the Worland family line back to settlers who came to American in 1662. Worlands all around the U.S.A. can trace their lineage back to John Worland, who came to America from Wales. At the family reunion we attended before our trip really got underway, relatives said since we would be traveling in that part of the country anyway, we needed to make Worland, Wyoming, an official destination.

Driving toward the Wyoming city, we were struck by the beauty of the area. That region might not top your priority list of travel destinations, but I can assure you that you would never regret any time spent there. When we arrived in Worland, we found a neat western town with a main street with many "mom and pop" stores.

It was great fun to see our family name on everything and meet so many nice people. Interestingly, there no longer is a single person bearing the last name of Worland living there today. We were the first real Worlands to be in the city for many years. In fact, our visit was deemed so newsworthy that we were the subject for a feature article that appeared in the *Northern Wyoming Daily News.*

We visited the local Washakie Museum, where we found that a lot of work had been done researching the community's founder, Charlie "Dad" Worland and his wife, Sadie. It was especially meaningful for the children to learn a little more about their heritage. We even had some fun pretending that we owned everything that in one way or another bore the name of Worland. For instance, when Bonny Jean saw a building bearing our name, she would comment, "That's our building? Cool!" The other children would share her excitement, shouting, "That's our name, that's our name!" whenever they saw it in print.

Georgia St. Clair, who runs the museum, was especially helpful in relating to us the history of the Worland family in the area, especially Charlie, whom David believes is a cousin of his great-great-grandfather. It was a pleasure to hear her talking about the city's history and the family — it sounded almost as if she had known them personally.

The folks in the city treated us wonderfully, especially since we became a bit of a novelty. The newspaper article described us as "six Georgia peaches" in a motorhome, but it was really very complimentary of our endeavor, explaining how the whole enterprise came about and detailing some of the high points of our travels.

It was really a memorable experience, walking around the town and looking in the windows of shops. We were strolling down Big Horn Avenue, glancing at what the stores offered, when we stopped in front of the Prairie Wear clothing shop. Even though it was past closing time, we jokingly knocked on the door to see if anyone would let us in. To our surprise, Pearl Decker, the shop owner, opened the door and let us take a look around. Craig has talked for a long time about wanting to go to the University of Wyoming in Laramie, so buying a U of W t-shirt delighted him. And partly because Mrs. Decker was so kind in letting us in "after hours," we each got a souvenir of our own.

Another person who went out of his way to make us feel welcome was Levi French, a man we met at Ranchito (a Mexican restaurant), who overflowed with bubbly enthusiasm. Our visit in Wyoming was refreshing, educational, and gratifying.

Celebrating the birthday of Mrs. Norman Vincent Peale's (Ruth) at the Guide Post Magazine office Carmel, New York.

The White House • Washington, DC

New York City • Broadway Play

Trapp Family Inn
Stowe, Vermont

WILLIAMSBURG
"Homeschooling Week"

Suzannah & Bonny Jean

Craig (hat) and Scott directing

From this lake at our home at
Hidden Hollow to . . .
Scott & Bubba, in Alaska
Alaska
Glacier plane trip
Mount McKinley, Alaska
Sally and David
Dog Sledding in Girdwood, Alaska

The Hawaiian sign for hang loose.

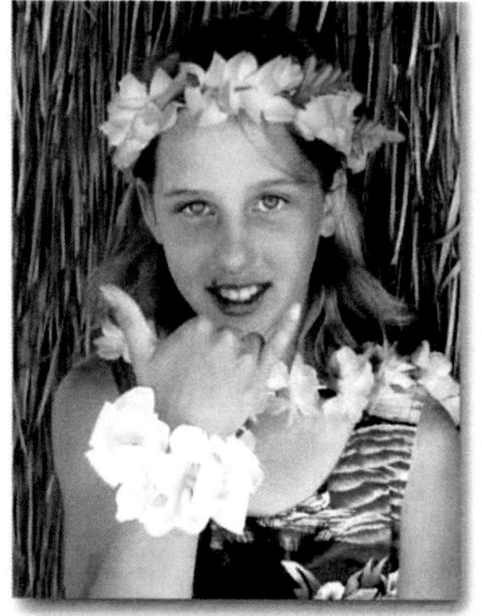

L-R: Suzannah, Scott, Bonny Jean, and Craig

PARADISE
COVE

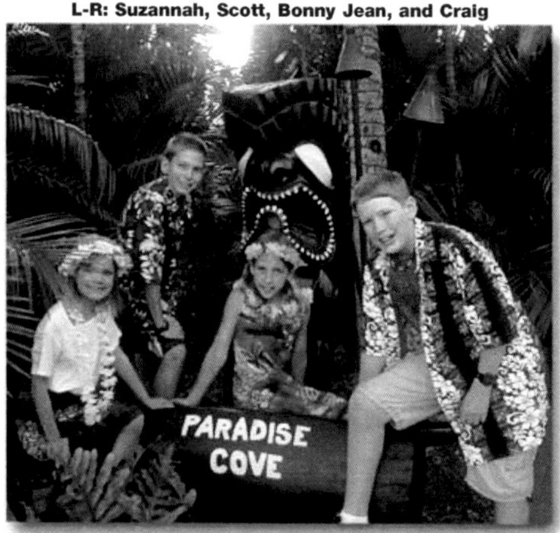

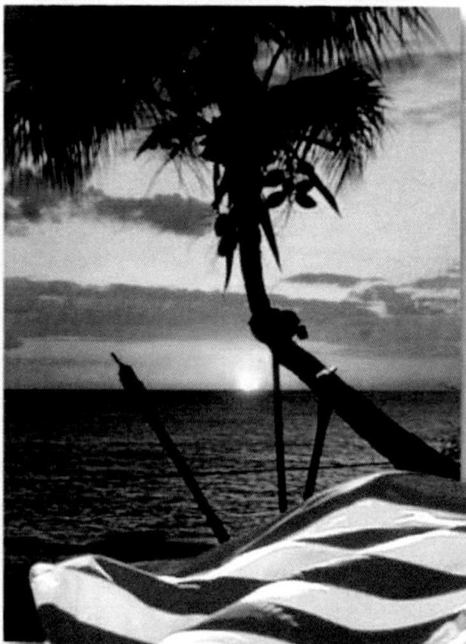

Bonny Jean

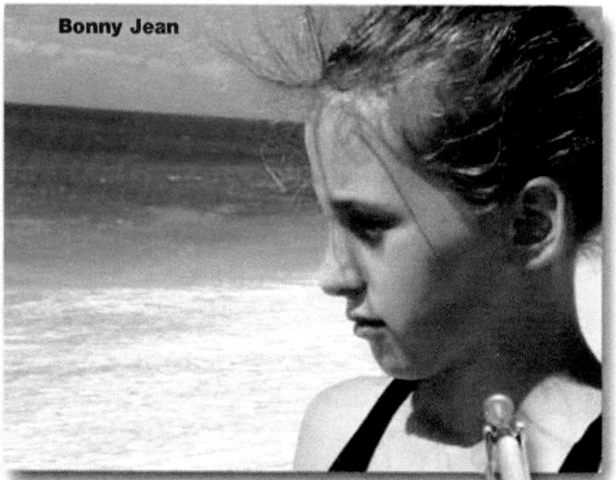

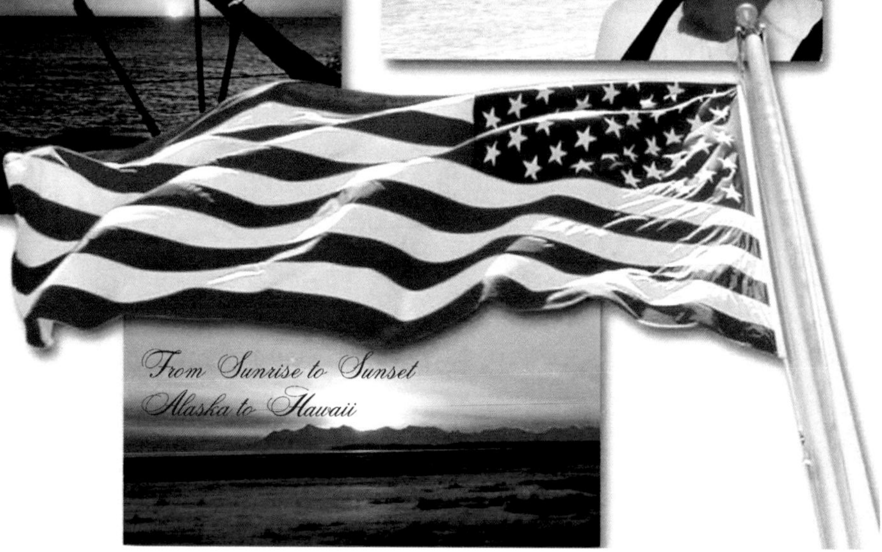
From Sunrise to Sunset
Alaska to Hawaii

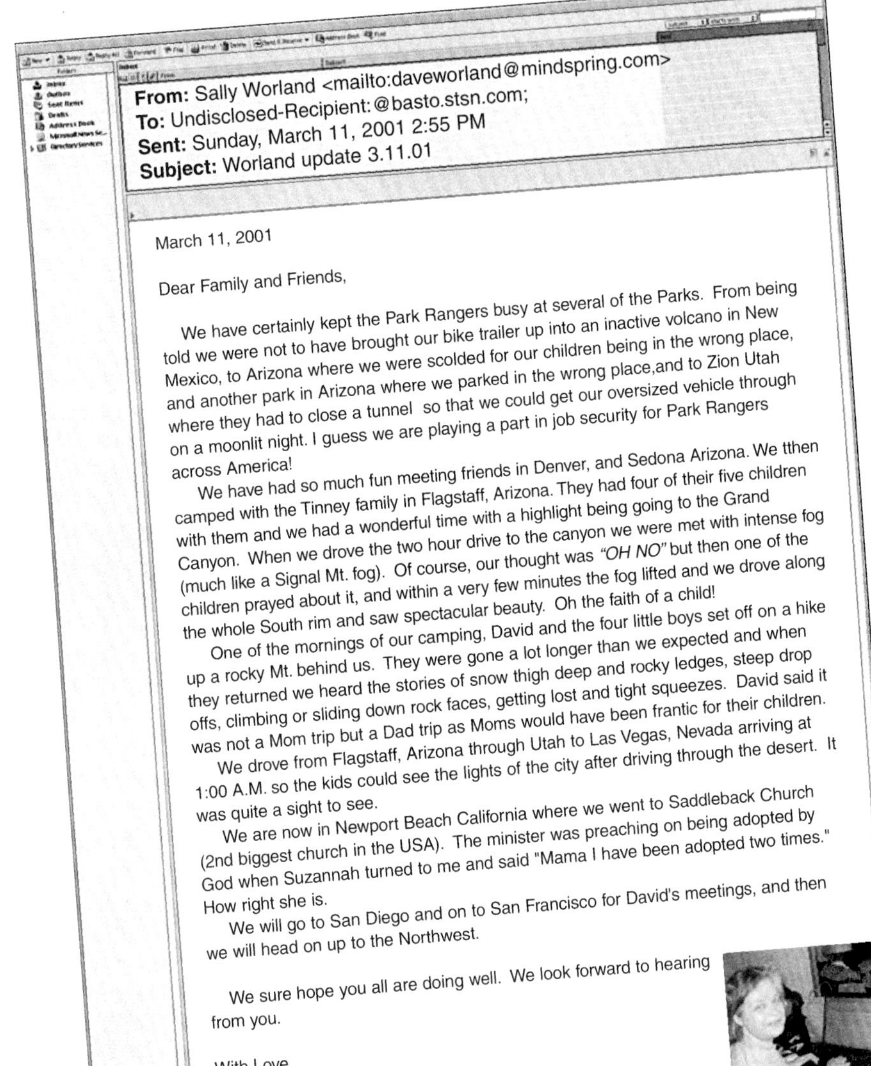

From: Sally Worland <mailto:daveworland@mindspring.com>
To: Undisclosed-Recipient:@basto.stsn.com;
Sent: Sunday, March 11, 2001 2:55 PM
Subject: Worland update 3.11.01

March 11, 2001

Dear Family and Friends,

We have certainly kept the Park Rangers busy at several of the Parks. From being told we were not to have brought our bike trailer up into an inactive volcano in New Mexico, to Arizona where we were scolded for our children being in the wrong place, and another park in Arizona where we parked in the wrong place,and to Zion Utah where they had to close a tunnel so that we could get our oversized vehicle through on a moonlit night. I guess we are playing a part in job security for Park Rangers across America!

We have had so much fun meeting friends in Denver, and Sedona Arizona. We tthen camped with the Tinney family in Flagstaff, Arizona. They had four of their five children with them and we had a wonderful time with a highlight being going to the Grand Canyon. When we drove the two hour drive to the canyon we were met with intense fog (much like a Signal Mt. fog). Of course, our thought was *"OH NO"* but then one of the children prayed about it, and within a very few minutes the fog lifted and we drove along the whole South rim and saw spectacular beauty. Oh the faith of a child!

One of the mornings of our camping, David and the four little boys set off on a hike up a rocky Mt. behind us. They were gone a lot longer than we expected and when they returned we heard the stories of snow thigh deep and rocky ledges, steep drop offs, climbing or sliding down rock faces, getting lost and tight squeezes. David said it was not a Mom trip but a Dad trip as Moms would have been frantic for their children.

We drove from Flagstaff, Arizona through Utah to Las Vegas, Nevada arriving at 1:00 A.M. so the kids could see the lights of the city after driving through the desert. It was quite a sight to see.

We are now in Newport Beach California where we went to Saddleback Church (2nd biggest church in the USA). The minister was preaching on being adopted by God when Suzannah turned to me and said "Mama I have been adopted two times." How right she is.

We will go to San Diego and on to San Francisco for David's meetings, and then we will head on up to the Northwest.

We sure hope you all are doing well. We look forward to hearing from you.

With Love,

Sally, David, Craig, Scott, Bonny Jean, and Suzannah

CHAPTER EIGHT

David Escapes from the Family Treadmill

So far in this book, my husband, David, has been kind of a "silent partner," and you have read the tour from my perspective, although he was as much a part of it as any of us. I would like to give him an opportunity to tell you about how he viewed the trip, and this might be a good time to do it. But first, I would like to give him a formal introduction:

David likes to joke that before we married we were "the perfect Christian couple. We met in Bible study at church, our parents on both sides are missionaries, we dated for fifteen years, and we knew each other perfectly." That is far from the case, as you will see as you read on, but I do think our methodical approach to courtship did give us the chance to resolve some critical issues before we exchanged our wedding vows — something that, unfortunately, isn't always the case for married couples.

I met David in 1975 when he applied for a job as a lifeguard and van driver for the YWCA where I worked. He had seen jobs posted for both the YMCA and YWCA, but being a young man who had a special interest in meeting people of the opposite sex, it made sense to him to apply to work at the YWCA.

I vividly remember the first time I saw him: He was covered with a reddish-colored beard, had long hair, and wore a flannel shirt and blue jeans. Since he would be working in my department, I conducted his interview and was impressed by how mature and "together" he seemed, so I hired him. Many years later, he still tells people that he had to fill out an application to meet me.

Although I was single, I honestly had no romantic notions about David at the time—or for quite a while afterward. He was several years younger than me, and David now teases that all the boys I dated had cars, and at that point his only mode of transportation was a bicycle.

Toward the end of the summer, just before he went off to college, David cut his hair and shaved off his beard, I remember thinking for the first time, *He's really a nice-looking man.* But then he left for college and I moved on with my life, thinking about him only occasionally.

I didn't see David for several years after that, and I assumed he had graduated from college and probably had gotten married. But one night I had a strong impression that I should try to contact him. I can't explain why (but I feel it was from God). I just knew that I should get back in touch with him. Since I had met his parents (Lee and Paul Worland) and gotten to know them fairly well before David left, I tried to act nonchalant, and I called his wonderful mom and I asked about his four brothers (Tom, Steve, Kevin, and Pete). We talked for a while and then I casually asked how David was doing, if he was married, and other information—indicating I just wanted to get updated.

When his mother told me that David was not married, I asked if I could have his address so I could write to him. She was glad to give it to me. After hanging up the phone, I immediately sat down and wrote David a letter. He was a wonderful person, but I wasn't sure where he was spiritually. I had a sense that perhaps there was a reason that both of us were still single, but I also was aware of the Bible's warning not to become unequally yoked in marriage with someone who did not share my faith in Christ.

I dropped the letter in the mail in November, but didn't hear back from David until March of 1982. I had to laugh when I finally received the reply from him. On the outside of the envelope, David had written, "Got your letter in November, wrote in December, lost it in January, found it in February, and mailed it in March." That, believe it or not, marked the real beginning of our courtship!

The following July, David came to Chattanooga, but he didn't tell me in advance. One afternoon he just appeared at my camp, standing near the chapel, which is located along the lake. It was quite a pleasant surprise for me. As I looked down at him from the chapel trail, I felt certain I was going to marry David some day.

One day in October of 1983, we were walking from a friend's house to my home. Still uncertain about David's spiritual commitment, I turned and asked him, "What is the most important thing in your life?" Without hesitation, he answered, "Knowing Jesus Christ as my Lord and Savior." Wow — what an answer to prayer that was for me!

It was on December 11 of that year — David's birthday — when we got around to determining that we wanted to spend the rest of our lives together. As a surprise, I showed up on David's doorstep, in High Point, North Carolina, to wish him a happy birthday. We had not yet admitted to one another that we were serious. My visit was a surprise for both of us as a friend of his had planned a birthday dinner party for him with a blind date. At the end of the date, the young woman asked him if she could see him again. He smiled and told her, "No, I don't think so. I'm getting ready to go home and ask a girl from Tennessee to marry me." And that's what he did.

We got married on May 12, 1984, at Signal Mountain Presbyterian Church. Our reception was held at Hidden Hollow, (where we live now), on a beautiful Spring afternoon. The fruit trees and dogwood trees were in full blossom and we even had a horse and carriage to bring us down the country lane. We went to New England for an extended honeymoon and spent three weeks really getting to know each other better, since our courtship had mostly been by long distance. So our return to New England in the fall of 2000 with our children was an especially poignant time for us.

A New Perspective of Their Father

Our trip provided a chance for the kids to see a different side of their dad. David has always led by strong example, but as we traveled the children caught glimpses of his softer side, even seeing instances of his own vulnerability. I think this was wonderful, because they could see that a strong man can still display sensitivity and emotion. By being able to see the many facets of their father, the children found him to be even more approachable than they had imagined.

Too often dads tend to communicate that they are all-powerful, that nothing phases them. But the kids quickly found that was not the case with David. For instance, he's claustrophobic. Living in the RV wasn't a problem, because there was adequate space and windows, but he couldn't have slept on a top bunk in the back of the motorhome. It would have been too confining for him.

In recounting our travels, my recollections have tended to focus on the fun we had and the incredible range of opportunities we were able to experience. David, however, tends to be more philosophical in how he looks at things and, of course, much of his time was consumed with his work responsibilities, even though he still had a lot of time to spend with the kids as well.

It is my desire that telling our story will challenge you to take time and consider how you could also engage in a unique, once-in-a-lifetime activity that could be forever etched in the hearts and lives of you and those you love, I want David to share his own perspectives on our travels together.

David Shares His Thoughts

What an incredible opportunity it was for us, over a year's time, to see all fifty states. Although it was an idea we had dreamed about for our family, we certainly could not have planned it—at least not in the way it came about. God clearly orchestrated the whole process, even the fact that Sally and I shared this dream in the first place. It was a real gift from Him, and definitely not something we in any way deserved or that He was in any way obligated to do for us.

Even though it would be easy to talk about the places we visited and the sights we enjoyed along the way, what hit me the hardest about the entire journey was that until we got away, I never realized how busy we are in our normal, day-to-day lives. Work, church activities, school, recreational sports, keeping a house maintained—they all consume so much of our time, and often we're not even aware of it.

The trip eliminated all of that busyness. It was interesting to have someone else worry about things like preparing food, for example. We did cook, but not as Sally does when we are home, so for the most part we relied on restaurants to do our food selection and preparation.

When we had mechanical breakdowns, which happened very rarely, it was a major ordeal. But the interesting thing was, life had to come to a stop for us then. At home, when a vehicle needs repair, we take it to the shop, switch to another vehicle, and life goes on. In a way, the breakdowns were welcomed because they did force us to pause and enjoy wherever we were and whatever we were doing.

In our everyday life, so much of our attention is focused on other people outside of the immediate family. When we left home and were hundreds or even thousands of miles away, all that had to be set aside. It was a very different experience for us, but the majority of our time and focus was concentrated on our family — on each other. It was interesting not to have to be focused with church friends, what was going on in school, or colleagues at work. We appreciate all of them, but the ability to redirect our attention to one another was an unexpected and very pleasant by-product of the trip.

People often ask about what it was like living in such close quarters, but traveling down the road in a thirty-one-foot RV affords everyone a lot of room, even with six people sharing the space. It's not like we had tried to make the trip in a car, an SUV, or a van. We really had a lot of room. There were two separate rooms in the motorhome, so if a time came when someone felt a need to be alone, they could go to another room for a while. And when we stayed at a campground, everyone spent most of the time outdoors anyway, so it wasn't as if we were confined to restricted living quarters twenty-four hours a day.

Trying to Mesh Schedules

No question, there were a few inconveniences. For instance, I like to get up early in the morning and there were many times when

I would sneak out of the RV to get a cup of coffee and read the newspaper, or whatever. We never got everyone's schedules perfectly aligned, so it was an interesting challenge to get our plans and agendas somewhat coordinated and maintain respect for one another's time and needs. Instead of competing, we tried to encourage the children to help one another with whatever they were trying to do.

This whole process taught us to communicate a lot better. We found that if you get upset with somebody, when you are spending the entire day in an RV, you can't just stuff it down and go to work, do schoolwork, or whatever. We all had to learn to deal with issues that arose among us.

I learned a lot about my boys in particular. We took the trip when they were at ages where their own personalities were beginning to evolve. I learned a lot about how they think, what they do, and generally the things that go on in their lives. We had a lot of opportunities to talk, share our true feelings, to reconcile differences, and salve hurts we had caused one another.

Basically, the trip stripped away all the busyness of life, all the pressures and outside distractions that the twenty-first-century family faces. We learned about teamwork, having to focus as a family to accomplish specific tasks. For me, much of the time was spent with phone calls, meetings and activities, and tasks to perform, so the family couldn't look to Dad to make all the decisions or handle all the details. Every night, for example, we had to look for a place to stay, whether it was a campground or hotel. Believe it or not, when you do that night after night, it takes a lot of coordination and planning.

As I reflected on it, it reminded me very much of what it must have been like many years ago when the early farmers worked on family farms. They would rise early each morning and talk about their plans for the day, and then determine what chores each member of the family needed to do. If there were problems, they would sit at the table and talk them through; if there were special joys, they would discuss those as well. They were very engaged in one another's lives—very close to one another, physically and emotionally. That is something I think that most contemporary families have lost.

Chilling Out At Mount Rushmore

We visited Mount Rushmore in April of 2001 during a swing back through South Dakota. As is typical of that region at that time of year, it was cold. But we loved our time there. Seeing the four presidents whose faces were carved into the mountainside — George Washington, Thomas Jefferson, Theodore Roosevelt, and Abraham Lincoln — was an amazing sight, of course. You can't fully appreciate the impact of those images simply from photographs. It has to be viewed, as they say, up close and personal.

But there were other aspects of the mountain that impressed us almost as much. The Great Hall of Flags, for example, was very noteworthy, displaying the flag of every U.S. state along the walkway as we approached the fabled mountain. Not only did it point with pride to the various states that form the great Union we call the United States, but it provided us with a visual representation of the year-long adventure we had been taking.

Every photo we had seen of the mountain sculptures was taken from the front, so it was a pleasant surprise for us to drive around from the back of the mountain and, as we turned toward the front, to see the profile of George Washington's face standing out in bold relief. We weren't expecting that, but it showed so clearly how much work had been invested in cutting — and blasting — away the many tons of stone.

Finally, as we gazed with wonder at the incredible view of this "mountain with the heads in it," we thought about how it had resulted from the labors of ordinary men engaged in doing extraordinary things. This wasn't a project accomplished by using hammer and chisel. It was such a tremendous undertaking, sculpting faces solely through the ability to properly set dynamite charges to remove only limited areas of stone. The tour guide explained how the workers of this massive project, who had never done anything like it before, simply got better as they had more opportunities to perform a very precise sculpture — with explosives.

Mount Rushmore is generally regarded as the creation of Gutzon Borglum, who envisioned and supervised much of the project, but we thought about the many men who contributed to this work, men whose names we will never know. Despite the anonymity of these courageous individuals — just simple men who joined their talents and skills to do a once-in-a-lifetime, exceptional endeavor — thousands of people from all around the world come each year to marvel at these awesome stone faces.

I thought of how, in a sense, the members of the Worland family could be described in a similar way. We were just six very ordinary people, given the opportunity to participate in a very extraordinary adventure —traversing the United States and taking in the wonders of each of the fifty states. Yes, this particular experience is not afforded to most people, but the extraordinary is within the reach of virtually anyone with imagination and determination.

Positives of Meeting Just Plain People

Another lasting impression I had from our trip was of the hundreds of people we met as we visited their cities and towns. In New England, for example, we stopped at a little café. The people there were so friendly, and after they saw our RV they wanted to know the story of our travels. They were eager to talk with us about what we were doing and why.

In the newspapers and TV newscasts, we hear so much about the negative side of the United States and the evil that exists everywhere. But the people we met during our travels were exceptional. I don't know if I can think of a single person who was not friendly toward us, whether it was a waitress, a hotel innkeeper, or even someone we met along the street.

There are a lot of people across America who are happy, enjoying each other and the work that they do. They seemed quite content with their lives and relationships — their own private worlds. While some of the people we met might not have acknowledged it if we had asked them, they were obviously taking great joy in what God had given to them.

The United States is not only diverse in terms of national and ethnic backgrounds, religions, and creeds, but it also boasts an awe-inspiring diversity in its geography. There were many times — more than we could remember — when we were literally speechless as we marveled at the beauty of God's creation in different parts of the country. Witnessing the majesty of His handiwork at times caused us to be overcome with amazement and thankfulness, whether it was a brilliant sunrise or glorious sunset; the vast, almost incomprehensible expanse of the Grand Canyon; the grandeur of the Rocky Mountains; the verdant vistas of the Pacific Northwest, or the spectacular hues of autumn in New England.

Results Far Exceeded Expectations

From a professional standpoint, the dozens of meetings I had throughout our trip had results beyond anything I had hoped to see.

Terry Parker, one of the founders of NCF, (in 1982), and I had begun working together in charitable foundation work in 1992. At the time, he had just left a law firm in Atlanta, and I had left a position as a banking executive in Chattanooga. While his energy was on a national scale, I was involved with local charitable work. Early in 2000, Terry and David Wills (CEO of NCF) approached me about the possibility of joining the NCF team with the sole purpose, at least initially, of helping to start Christian community foundations around the United States.

The people with whom I had met had already expressed interest in working with NCF, so I wasn't making "sales calls." Professional financial advisers we work with around the country had referred these individuals and foundations to us. They were excited about being able to interact with someone to learn how to channel the resources within their cities and towns to provide more effectively for local needs and, at the same time, truly make a difference for eternity.

As a Christian, I am impressed all the more with what it means to be an ordinary person called to be involved in the work of an extraordinary God. During the numerous meetings I had with dedicated men and women in more than forty cities as we journeyed across the U.S.A., I was so encouraged to see the vision they had for their communities, and how deeply they wanted to make a difference through their local foundations.

Sometimes I would meet with an individual 'champion,' someone with a dream to get a foundation started locally. We would brainstorm, trying to envision how this could come about and what would be necessary to make it happen. After trying to stretch their vision and offering some general direction, we then would develop a plan of action to help them carry out their intentions.

If the key leader had already formed a steering committee, I would meet with them and assist them in working through basic strategic areas we have found are essential for any local foundation to serve its constituency effectively. Rather than trying to answer all of their questions, I could connect them with people in other parts of the country who might be better equipped to provide the answers based on their own experience.

At times an operational board was already in place, so I would work with the foundation in the process of hiring staff, mentoring the new executive director, and helping to provide direction and leadership in whatever areas it was needed.

In each case, I was able to show how to more effectively meet the charitable giving needs of individuals in their communities who had been very blessed materially. In addition, when I worked with large church and community ministries, sometimes I met with their major donors and showed them ways for achieving whatever their personal giving goals happened to be. Obviously, these ministries hoped these meetings would result in the donors giving more to their own projects, or at least to show them how to make more capital available that they eventually could release to their ministry and other works within the kingdom of God.

The fact that I was able to go to forty-three cities and meet with many incredibly committed and generous people, without having to spend many weeks away from my family, was an unbelievable blessing. Going on the road with Sally and our kids, traveling from city to city to meet with these leaders, and seeing so much of our nation in the process worked out extremely well. We could not have expected or asked for a better outcome, professionally or personally.

In this book we point to various ways in which we believe the Lord has clearly directed our lives – such as how Sally and I met and eventually got married; how we adopted Suzannah; and how He provided the means by which we could take our journey around the U.S.A. At the opening of the book, Sally told you about our encounter with the snowplow as we tried to maneuver through the snowy night on the Bighorn Mountains. There is no question in our minds that, in one way or another, that snowplow was God intervening to guide us to safety.

But it wasn't always so dramatic. Throughout the trip, even in small details, we observed evidence of the Lord at work, as if He were traveling right along with us. And, as people who believe in God's omnipresence, we know He did accompany us on the trip.

3rd bike rack

FINALLY OUR BIKE TRAILER

Scott and David at Washington, DC US Treasury

Suzannah and David

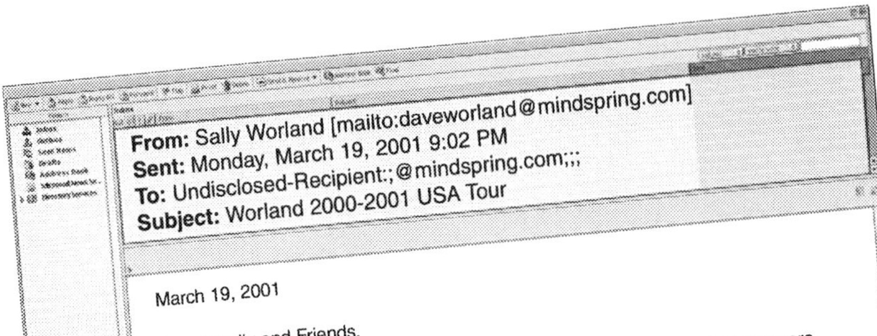

From: Sally Worland [mailto:daveworland@mindspring.com]
Sent: Monday, March 19, 2001 9:02 PM
To: Undisclosed-Recipient:;@mindspring.com;;;
Subject: Worland 2000-2001 USA Tour

March 19, 2001

Dear Family and Friends,

As our family sat and visited with our friend Semore (Sam in English) we were amazed to hear the stories of how he escaped Eastern Africa and smuggled his children to freedom. We met Sam about two years ago, in California, as he was our taxi driver and we developed a friendship and wanted our children to meet the man we had had the good fortune to get to know. He has educated both of his sons and they are both working on their Master's. He has met his goal of bringing them to freedom and letting them get a good education. What an inspiration he is.

We have really enjoyed camping and had a wonderful time in a beautiful campground in Felton, California. It was right in the middle of the Redwood Forrest. It was so neat to be in the midst of these big beautiful trees. We all enjoyed bike riding through the woods beside the river. In one place Craig and I were riding along a narrow and curvy path with railroad tracks on one side and the river on the other down a steep embankment. If you took your eyes off the narrow path you could have easily fallen. (Do you hear a sermon coming?)

We went to San Francisco where we went over the Golden Gate Bridge and went on Lombard Street , the curviest road in America. Of course, they haven't seen the W Road up Signal Mt. We ate at Fisherman's Wharf and went to see and hear the clang, clang, clang of the trolley. We are now in San Jose, where David has a big meeting tomorrow. We have been doing our schooling this evening as I needed David here to make sure the math teacher was correct on some of the work! It is bad when the students are smarter than the teacher. Oh, I know it doesn't take much.

It is hard to believe that we are coming to the last month of our travels. We will go to Alaska early April, and then after we get home if everything goes as planned we will go to Hawaii which will make all fifty states. Wow, what a year. We have saved our Skymiles from Delta for years and will use them as we take vacation time for these two states. We decided while we are on a roll to try and do it all. I believe the children's desire for travel has been increased as Bonny Jean said she wanted to take her children on a trip around the world. It has been wonderful, but we are all a little homesick and look forward to being back home and seeing family and friends.

Keep the news coming with your e-mails. Take care.

Love,

Sally, David, Craig, Scott, Bonny Jean, and Suzannah

CHAPTER NINE

The Nicest People You Would Ever Want to Meet

When you take an extended trip around the United States, it would seem quite typical to focus on the visual delights we were so blessed to see each day. Our nation truly is "America the Beautiful." But next to the priceless experience of sharing twelve months of our lives as a family in the close proximity of a motor home, probably the second most significant aspect of our travels was comprised of the wonderful people we met along the way.

On many occasions, we were guests of David's clients for a meal. The warmth of their hospitality, flowing from their love of the Lord, was unforgettable. And these were not all well-to-do philanthropists. In fact, some of the most memorable people with whom we had the opportunity to spend time had only limited means, but their hearts for reaching out to others in their community knew no limit. That was often reflected in the hospitality they extended to our family.

A very special encounter, one that truly was unexpected, occurred after we had attended a worship service at Dr. Tony Evans' church, Oak Cliff Bible Fellowship in Dallas, Texas. Dr. Evans had given a very practical message on learning how to wait on the Lord. Recalling the years we had prayed and planned for our U.S.A. trip, we all could relate to the principles he taught in the sermon.

When we walked back to our RV that Sunday, we found a note from a family in the church. They were homeschooling their children and had seen our sign, "4 Road Scholars: Home Schoolers Traveling the U.S.A.," on our RV. In the note they indicated they would like to talk with us. They left their telephone number, so we called and offered to meet them at an IHOP restaurant not far from the church.

When they arrived at the restaurant, we saw that they were an African-American family, also with four children. We had the most wonderful visit with them while we enjoyed a meal together.

After we were finished, we all went into our RV and continued our conversation. When we were ready to leave, they asked if we could form a circle and pray together for the rest of our trip. It warmed my heart to see our children's white hands holding the little black hands of the other children in our prayer circle, united in one faith, acknowledging there are no color, ethnic, or national barriers to Jesus. I remember thinking, *"I hope our children always feel joined to other people who share their faith, regardless of their different backgrounds."*

What a blessing that was to have people we had just met — new friends — offering to help undergird our travels in prayer. We felt so strengthened spiritually by the times we spent together with brothers and sisters in Christ. The instant bond we experienced was evidence of the reality of the Lord in all of our lives. Even within individual churches, this unity is not always experienced, unfortunately, but our time with this family was just one example of occasions when we saw what can happen if we are just willing to reach out and put differences aside, whatever they may be.

After that impromptu visit, David, the children, and I went to the John F. Kennedy Memorial and Cowboys Stadium, the home of the Dallas Cowboys football team. As you can guess, the boys insisted that we go there. Both of those stops were fascinating, a curious blend of history and athletics, but neither compared to our time earlier that day when twelve strangers joined hands in prayer in our RV's small living room.

A Snowy Sunday in Kansas City

We had a similar experience one Sunday in Kansas City, Kansas when we visited Harvest Church. David and I have always tried to teach our children not to have any prejudice toward other races, but this offered an even stronger opportunity to reinforce that principle.

Saturday evening, a strong snow and ice storm had blown through Kansas City so we found refuge in a hotel rather than trying to find a campground. The kids and I were going to remain in the city for the better part of ten days anyway since David was getting ready to fly to Atlanta for a conference. We had selected the hotel because it seemed safe and in a good area for our extended stay until David's return.

After we checked in, we looked out the window and saw a church that we thought might be good to visit. Because of the icy roads, we didn't want to drive far the next morning so this also seemed very convenient. We went to the hotel's front desk and asked the clerks, "Do you know anything about the church across the street?"

The clerks replied, whispering almost apologetically, "Well, it's primarily African-American." We didn't know whether they responded that way because they saw we were from Georgia or what, but in any case they seemed to think that would be a concern for us. We assured them it didn't matter to us whether it was Caucasian, African-American, Asian or what — we just wanted to know if they had any other information about the church, including the worship schedule.

On Sunday morning we went through our usual routine in getting ready for church, putting on our designated outfits, and then were able to drive slowly over to the church. When we arrived, several young men who had umbrellas met us at the door and offered to help us into the church. It was such a nice reception that we just knew we were going to enjoy our time there. Even though the church was very large, we obviously stood out as one of the few families in attendance that was white. That obviously made no difference to the church members, however. As we walked in, people began hugging us, telling us they were so glad we had come, and they made us feel as though we were a part of their family, which we were, as brothers and sisters in Christ, even though we were from a different part of the country.

Before the service we met the minister and explained about our travels, mentioning that David would be leaving us in Kansas City for about ten days. Without hesitating, the pastor said, "David, since you're going to be gone, we want Sally to know that she can call on us, and we'll take care of her and the family if she needs anything at all."

The worship service was terrific; very uplifting and soundly based on God's Word. We couldn't have been more delighted that we were able to visit the church that morning. Afterward, we found out that more than ninty percent of the people in the church were comprised of single mothers and their children, but they all had given generously from their hearts to purchase the building, which had been part of a shopping mall. This former retail center had been transformed into the worship center, classrooms, and a beautiful big gymnasium, and as we understood it, was largely paid for with the resources of single parents.

It happened to be Super Bowl Sunday so we were invited to come back that night for a Super Bowl party the church was hosting in the gym. The pastor explained they had a large projection screen for viewing the game, and chairs were even set up so people could sit on opposite sides if they wanted to so they could root for their favorite teams.

We did go to the church that evening; as we entered the gymnasium, people all over started waving at us and telling us how glad they were that we had come back. Our only problem was in deciding which invitation to "sit by us" we should accept. Rarely have we ever felt so loved in a church.

Also in Kansas City, we had the opportunity to enjoy an extended visit with Ken Canfield of the National Center for Fathering. He and I serve together on a committee on the family for the National Christian Foundation, and I have grown to have great respect for him.

Finding a "Faithful Remnant" Everywhere

During our time in New England, we surmised that there did not seem to be nearly the evangelical push as we were accustomed to encountering in the South. There seem to be fewer churches in that part of the country. One day while we were in New Hampshire, however, we were spending some time at a shopping mall when a woman walked up to Bonny Jean and started a very unexpected conversation.

The woman told us that she could tell by Bonny Jean's countenance, even though my daughter was only nine years old at the time, that she was a Christian. This woman, probably in her early sixties, said she desperately needed to talk to another Christian. We stood there for a long while and had a wonderful visit. She gave us some information about her family and some problems they were having. She then explained how much they all needed our prayers.

It was a time when we all were encouraged, marveling at how God had brought us together as strangers, except for the bond we had in Jesus Christ. It was a meaningful time for Bonny Jean, too, showing her the importance of being a good witness — even when she's not saying anything.

Meeting a Former Pitching Star

In Colorado Springs, one of the wonderful people we met was Dave Dravecky, the former major league baseball pitcher with the San Francisco Giants, whose career came to a premature end in 1989 after battling bone cancer in his left (pitching) arm. The entire arm had to be removed in 1991. Dave has established a nonprofit ministry, called Dave Dravecky's Outreach of Hope, dedicated to encouraging people suffering with cancer, amputation, and other serious diseases. He and my husband met for quite a while, discussing strategies for fulfilling the vision he has for his work.

Dave was very gracious with our children, and Scott was especially thrilled to meet him because he had done a project on Dave's life for school the year before. Dave was every bit as genuine as he seemed to be in his books, and it was fun to become acquainted with him and what God has called him to do "post-baseball."

While we were in Colorado Springs, we also took the time to tour the Focus on the Family facilities and get a sense of the scope of what that organization is doing on behalf of families and traditional values. I work with Mac MacQuiston, one of the top executives with Focus on the Family, on the family committee for the National Christian Foundation, so it was enlightening to see firsthand some of the initiatives with which Mac is involved.

Getting Reacquainted with Family

Memorable times we spent with people during our travels were not limited to people we had not met previously. In Hawaii, we had an enjoyable visit with my cousin, Maria O'Brien, and her husband, John, whom I had not seen for about fifteen years. She is a talented lady, who has served as medical director for a number of Hawaii-based TV shows, providing medical expertise whenever needed, including *Hawaii 5-0.* Maria even had one of the cars that had been used in that police drama.

She also had served as Loretta Young's personal nurse for a number of years so it was fun to spend time with her and listen to her stories about experiences in the entertainment world.

We were specially blessed at other times when family members and friends would take the time to join us for several days while we were in different parts of the country. Sometimes, they would just organize their vacations so at some point their travels would intersect with ours. These visits definitely helped to ease any homesickness we were encountering.

Girls in a Redwood Tree
California

Biking in Yosemite

Bonny Jean

Riding at Lost Valley Ranch, Colorado

Craig

Scott

Suzannah

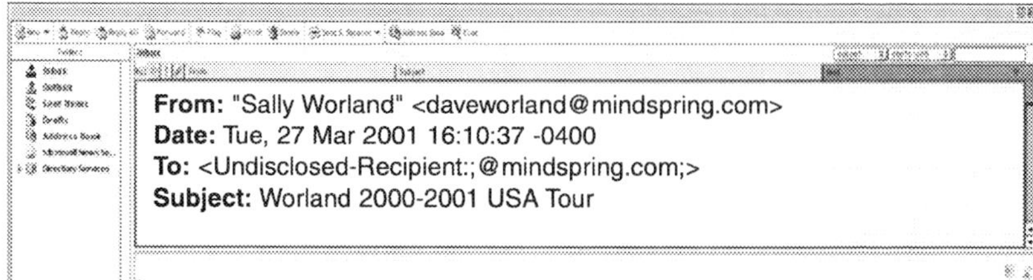

From: "Sally Worland" <daveworland@mindspring.com>
Date: Tue, 27 Mar 2001 16:10:37 -0400
To: <Undisclosed-Recipient:;@mindspring.com;>
Subject: Worland 2000-2001 USA Tour

March 27, 2001

Dear Family and Friends,

I do believe digital pictures need to be labeled fiction or non-fiction. David has bought a digital camera, and has he ever had fun. He shows me how he can make the mountain bigger, put a rainbow wherever he wants it, make the picture clearer, and just overall change the original photo. Well, I have expressed my "antiquated opinion" quite often and decided that I had better watch my words when I realized David could replace me with Julia Roberts!

It seems I also am having to take back my opinion on California. I have mainly been in the Southern part of California and have not always had the fondest thoughts of the State. We have now been in Yosemite and Northern California and both are absolutely beautiful. It is good to mature in our thoughts, isn't it? The children keep reminding David and me that we are maturing in other ways as we both have gotten more gray hair on this adventure. Anyway, I do know that all of us have seen beauty in every state and love the diversity of this great nation.

Well we could stay in a perfectly good campground or hotel tonight but after reading that nearly one third of RV'ers have stayed in a Wal-Mart parking lot ,as they are very camper friendly, we are going to stay at a Wal-Mart. Now I know most of you are envious so if you want to meet us, we will plan to be somewhere in the Seattle area.The children are more excited about Wal-Mart than Yosemite. Isn't it true that children always have as much fun with the box as the toy? They want us to stay in a 24-hour one so that they can aisle shop all night. I wonder if they provide showers? We will have to let you know how it goes.

Yesterday, we went to the biggest sea cave in the world, and it was full of sea lions. It was located near Florence, Oregon. We went down an elevator for over 200 feet and as we went lower the smell of sea creatures got stronger and stronger. By the time the elevator door opened, we all felt we needed clothes pins. We really enjoyed seeing the sea lions but because of the odor they didn't have to worry about our hanging around too long. Of course, after no showers tonight the Wal-Mart might feel the same way about us.

We have stayed in some neat campgrounds in California and Oregon. We are still helping the park rangers with job security. We were staying on a bay in California and the kids wanted to swim in the bay. I had ridden my bike to the camp store and on the way back I saw a sign by the boat dock that said "no swimming, contaminated water." Assuming they meant the gasoline from the boats was the problem, I did not think much about it but decided to ask anyway. They said that the whole bay was contaminated because of all the runoff from the rain. I took off on my bike to warn David, and you guessed it, I found four empty bikes at the swimming shore and found David and the kids at the showers. They had been swimming when a park ranger came along and told David the water was contaminated and to get the children out immediately. He rushed them to the showers, and they scrubbed like never before. Why they didn't have a sign at the swimming beach we don't know.

The children are preparing for another oral book report. I am trying to help them learn some about public speaking so with their index cards in hand they must keep this report to five to seven minutes. As I shared before, their last reports lasted close to two hours with David falling asleep twice. They will give these on Thursday.

David has had some great meetings and seems to be accomplishing so much. We have the opportunity to have dinner in the homes of some wonderful people associated with NCCF.

Well, as always our best to each of you. Please keep the e-mails coming as it is great hearing from you all.

With Love, Sally, David, Craig, Scott, Bonny Jean, and Suzannah

CHAPTER TEN

You Can't Drive There From Here

The RV served us well throughout our travels in the continental U.S., but it had two limitations: It wasn't suited to traverse thousands of miles of terrain across Canada to Alaska, and it could not conquer the formidable challenge of the Pacific Ocean. So we elected to take the next best alternative: we flew to the 49th and 50th states, the final "requirements" for our goal of literally going to each of the fifty states. These trips were David's vacation and not work related.

In April 2001, we flew from Seattle, Washington, to Anchorage, Alaska, where we rented a van and drove to Girdwood in the Chattoog Mountains. We stayed in the "junior suite" at the Alyeska Resort, which is surrounded by awesome, snow-capped mountains. The room was nice, but David and I realized that as our travels were winding down, the children's tolerance level was being pushed pretty far; they were looking forward to getting back home where they each could have their space. (One of the most profound lessons we gained on the trip was that when someone reaches the point where they need some space, you need to give it to them — immediately!)

But outdoors in the Great Land, as natives like to call their state, was a different story. Rather than "Great Land," my nickname for it would have been winter wonderland. As we had been anticipating the trip to Alaska, one of the activities we looked forward to most was dog sledding. It was disappointing to discover that at the time we were there, most companies had already ceased their dogsled operations for the season. However, we were so happy when we found a group near the resort that had not yet closed.

What an exhilarating experience it was to ride through the woods, over the fields, through beautiful snow, and gaze at the majestic mountain peaks as we were pulled along in the sleds. Each of the children got to "mush" the dogs, which they thought was great.

But being hauled along by a team of huskies was just the start. Next came the snow skiing and snowboarding. As a lifelong Southerner undertaking these "up North" activities, two adages came to my mind: "Ignorance is bliss" and "You can't teach an old dog new tricks." Many years ago I had done a little bit of skiing, but it was essentially an exercise in proving the existence of gravity. I had never taken a lesson.

In those years past, I had advanced to the point of being able to go down some fairly moderate trails, but when David and I made the wise decision to take a beginning ski lesson, I found I had to relearn almost everything. So I spent all day trying to master the basics on the "bunny slope," while I watched our four children — who had received lessons from the get-go — progress wonderfully from one slope to another with increasing degrees of difficulty.

Then, while I continued to slide gingerly around my beginner's hill, the children moved on to snowboarding. They took some lessons for this as well, and soon the boys decided it was their favorite. What a thrill to see our next generation doing so well after having the advantage of basic lessons from the start.

I think this is a principle that fits whether you're dealing with some form of frozen water or pursuits that are totally different. If your children are obviously interested in a new sport or hobby, it's a great idea to provide them with good coaching and teaching from the beginning. It's much easier to learn something correctly from the start than to try to learn something all over and unlearn bad habits.

This applies in the spiritual realm as well, where too often new followers of Jesus Christ don't get the proper coaching or teaching to get them off to a good start in their walk with God. Somehow we seem to assume that their simple appearance when the church doors open is sufficient for healthy spiritual growth, but consider that Jesus invested Himself primarily in the lives of twelve men, twenty-four hours a day, seven days a week for three years. It would seem that a similar kind of focused, consistent spiritual training would benefit all of us as well — with young believers having an opportunity to get help from the start.

Back at the slopes, I did get to offer some "coaching" of my own later in the day when I exhorted our youngest child on the importance of knowing when to come in from the cold. Suzannah had complained about her feet freezing, so I took her indoors and discovered that she had slipped out of her snow boots while building a snowman; her feet were soaking wet. When I removed her wet socks, I found that one foot was extremely cold. It concerned me that she might have suffered some degree of frostbite, especially when she began crying as I tried to warm up the foot.

Finally, her foot warmed up and the pain went away, much to our mutual relief. When I asked Suzannah why she had not said anything earlier about her feet being so cold, her reply was understandable: "I was having so much fun, I didn't want to stop playing."

Cavorting in the snow was fun, but we also enjoyed another day when we had the opportunity to soar above the snow. We had seen nothing but snowfall and clouds during our entire time in Alaska until a day when we planned to take a plane ride over the glaciers. It turned out to be a spectacular, sunbathed day, and our view from the plane was magnificent. We saw blue glaciers that were just breathtaking in their beauty, along with crevices that were at least a thousand feet deep. We passed over Prince William Sound, the Turnagan Arm, Lake George, fjords (where glaciers meet the Pacific Ocean), saw glaciers "calving" (breaking apart), and buffalo roaming wild. What a feast for the eyes that was!

Majestic Mountain, Hidden by Fog

Next we drove about 250 miles to Talkeetna in south central Alaska, the location of the best view of Mount McKinley. But as we neared the area, we found clouds again. The mountain is 20,320 feet high, but on the particular day we were in that region, we could hardly see any of it. Fog, we were told, had enshrouded the mountain for about three weeks. If someone hadn't pointed and assured us there was a lofty mountain in the distance, we wouldn't have known for sure.

Someone in the family suggested that we pray, asking God if He couldn't do something about this problem — as we had done when we visited the Grand Canyon — so that's what we did. Actually, we called on Bonny Jean to say the prayer, asking the Lord to somehow move the clouds. However her prayer was a little different — she asked that the mountain would move! Well, I suppose that shows the faith of a child. Thankfully, God understood the intent of the prayer and left Mount McKinley where it had been for many centuries, which I'm sure was a relief to mapmakers around the world! Instead, He lifted the fog and gave us a truly spectacular view of the famous American peak. We will never forget that sight or the example of how integrally God is involved in the details of everyday life, even banishing fog when necessary.

While we were marveling at that grand, snow-capped mountain, two young men walked up, and we struck up a conversation. Sasha had climbed almost to the top of Mount McKinley and planned to try it again, while Mark was preparing to climb Mount Hunter, another majestic peak that stands next to Mount McKinley. Craig and Scott, as expected, listened wide-eyed and intently as the two fellows talked about some of their incredible experiences. I could almost see the wheels turning in our boys' minds as they imagined having similar adventures of their own.

It was wonderful to pray a prayer of thanksgiving with them before we parted ways. Afterward, wanting to remind Craig and Scott that we dearly desired their regular participation in our family for many years to come, we pointed out that it would be possible for them to experience many exciting times exploring God's creation without having to move so far away.

One of the best aspects of this trip was that since David had no foundation meetings planned for this area, he actually had a chance to relax and unwind. Like many dedicated workers, he sometimes finds it hard to separate work from vacation. It was a "timeout" he really needed.

We flew back to the lower forty-eight on April 7 and headed for Spokane, Washington, where David had a meeting scheduled with a group interested in establishing a local foundation. Knowing that our unique odyssey would be ending within weeks, we began to feel a twinge of regret, but at the same time our eagerness for returning home as we had known it — until the past twelve months — was beginning to grow.

Forty-Nine Down, One to Go!

There remained just one more state on our itinerary, the Aloha State. In early May, we packed up and headed for Hawaii, boarding a flight that originated in Chattanooga, changing planes in Atlanta, and then flying nonstop to Honolulu. We knew this was the final stop on our adventure and we felt a great sense of accomplishment in knowing that upon arrival there, we would have reached our goal of being together in each of the fifty states. I thought back over the twenty-three years since I had first acted on the desire to save frequent flyer points from Delta Airlines – even though at the time I was thoroughly enjoying single life – so that one day my hoped-for family and I would see the U.S.A. By nature I'm a planner and a dreamer, but when plans and dreams become reality, they are still unbelievable and so exciting.

When we arrived in Oahu the evening of May 10, we were assured it would be very easy to find our hotel, which was located just a few minutes away from the airport. Those "few minutes" turned into an hour until we finally stopped a policeman who tried to guide us by using his cell phone to call the hotel for specific directions. Finally, a bit frustrated that the instructions he received for locating the hotel still seemed vague, he said, "Just let me take you there." We thought it was very impressive to have a police escort on our first night in Hawaii to wrap up our itinerary.

But even armed with his cell phone, the officer discovered that finding the hotel was a challenge for him as well. We followed him, but every few minutes he would stop to use the phone again and recheck the directions. He stopped at one hotel but quickly determined that was not the right one so we resumed the procedure of "cell phone and follow."

Finally, he walked back to our car and with a wry smile told us that he finally discovered that the name of our hotel had changed so we actually had driven past it several times! He returned to his car, and we obediently followed him once more, hopeful that this was not one more wild goose chase. A few minutes later — about midnight — we indeed arrived at our destination, right in the downtown area. Not only was it late according to Hawaiian clocks, but we also were having to deal with a nine-hour time change from home.

Our travails for the night weren't quite over, however. As we checked in, we were politely informed that the hotel staff had already assigned our reserved, adjoining rooms to someone else. As I stood there at the hotel's front desk, wearily trying to decide how I should react to this perplexing development, the Lord's Spirit kept my spirit in check, and I remained calm. Then, even before we could voice any protest, the desk clerk said, "Let me check on something." He returned and announced that he was going to give us a "fat room" (which he explained means "really nice") for the same price as our original reservation. He directed us to one of the top floors in the hotel, and we discovered we were in a two-bedroom suite, complete with kitchen and windows all around the front and side, giving us an unbelievable view of the city and the ocean from the rooms and the balcony.

We had ended up with a presidential suite, a room that would have cost $545 a night if we had paid the established rate! Not only did we receive the very best accommodations available at a fraction of the cost, but we also were able to buy groceries and cook our own meals, which helped tremendously in dealing with the high cost of food on the island. This kind of happy "mistake" occurred three times during our trip around the country, in which the hotel got the reservations wrong, and we wound up getting much better rooms for the same daily rate. But this, on the final leg of our trip, was by far the most extravagant. In contrast to our time at the Residence Inn while David attended meetings at the Ritz Carlton, this time we were invited to stay at the Ritz. Yes, we indeed had been given a FAT room!

The next morning, our view from the windows of our suite was breathtaking: whitecaps slowly moving toward land, waves crashing on the shore, sand glistening in the sunlight. Without stepping outside our room, we were seeing the island of Oahu from a perspective that few people have the privilege to enjoy. We certainly didn't deserve such special treatment, but it was as if God were putting a special punctuation on the end of our journey, saying, "Here, children, I think you will really like this!"

We took in many of the popular sites on Oahu, touring the pineapple fields, the Diamond Head crater, Paradise Cove (where we enjoyed a luau), watching fire dancing and even trying hula dancing ourselves. We swam in the ocean at the Banzai Pipeline, went snorkeling, and took a small plane to the big island of Hawaii to spend a day enjoying the natural beauty, including the rain forest and the volcanoes.

Finally, as our days in the beautiful island state drew to a close, I realized that my dream had been transformed into "mission accomplished." While the individual experiences we had in each state made the trip worthwhile in themselves, it seemed to both David and me that our daily lives back in Georgia would never again seem as routine. We felt a deep sense of gratitude to the National Christian Foundation for making it possible for us to engage in such a unique adventure as well as family and friends, who also supported us in doing "something different."

"Mush" Dog sledding in Alaska

"Snow Woman"
by Bonny Jean

Aleyeska Resort

Rain Forest on the Big Island, Hawaii

Mothers Day in Hawaii

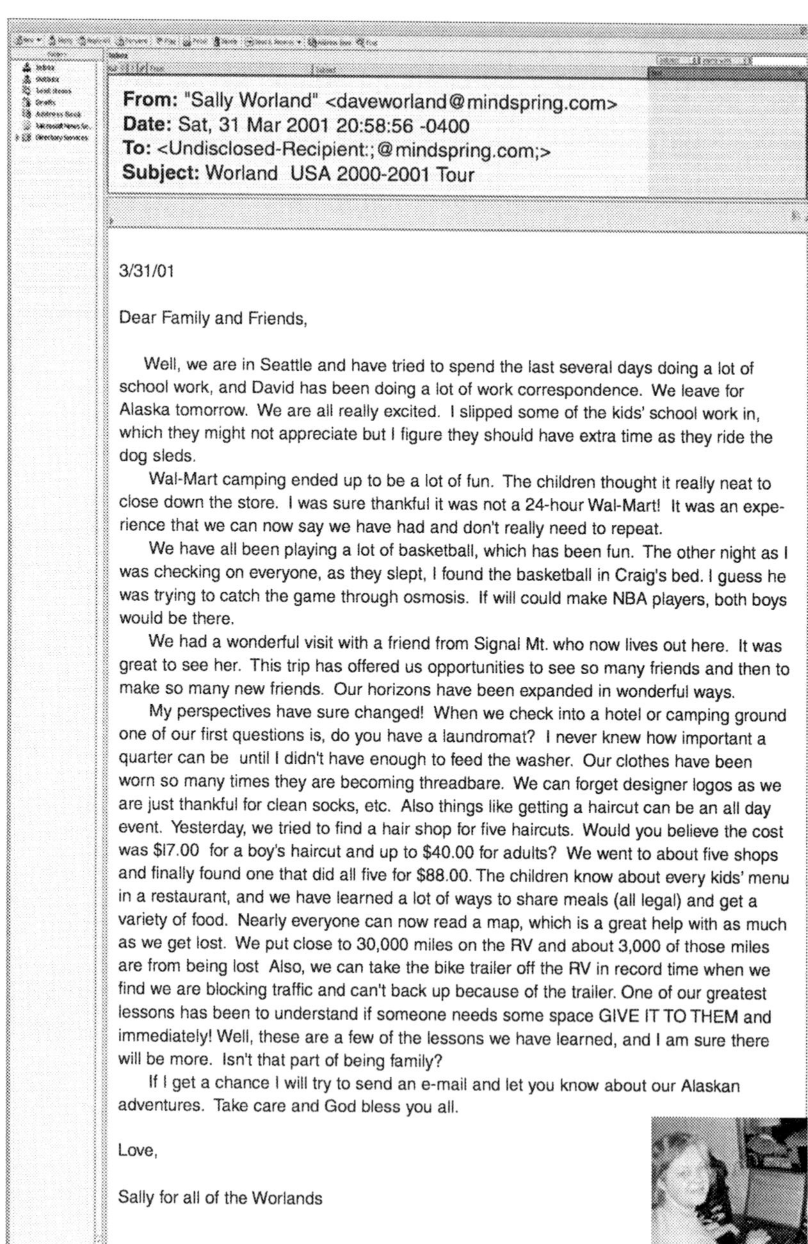

From: "Sally Worland" <daveworland@mindspring.com>
Date: Sat, 31 Mar 2001 20:58:56 -0400
To: <Undisclosed-Recipient:;@mindspring.com;>
Subject: Worland USA 2000-2001 Tour

3/31/01

Dear Family and Friends,

Well, we are in Seattle and have tried to spend the last several days doing a lot of school work, and David has been doing a lot of work correspondence. We leave for Alaska tomorrow. We are all really excited. I slipped some of the kids' school work in, which they might not appreciate but I figure they should have extra time as they ride the dog sleds.

Wal-Mart camping ended up to be a lot of fun. The children thought it really neat to close down the store. I was sure thankful it was not a 24-hour Wal-Mart! It was an experience that we can now say we have had and don't really need to repeat.

We have all been playing a lot of basketball, which has been fun. The other night as I was checking on everyone, as they slept, I found the basketball in Craig's bed. I guess he was trying to catch the game through osmosis. If will could make NBA players, both boys would be there.

We had a wonderful visit with a friend from Signal Mt. who now lives out here. It was great to see her. This trip has offered us opportunities to see so many friends and then to make so many new friends. Our horizons have been expanded in wonderful ways.

My perspectives have sure changed! When we check into a hotel or camping ground one of our first questions is, do you have a laundromat? I never knew how important a quarter can be until I didn't have enough to feed the washer. Our clothes have been worn so many times they are becoming threadbare. We can forget designer logos as we are just thankful for clean socks, etc. Also things like getting a haircut can be an all day event. Yesterday, we tried to find a hair shop for five haircuts. Would you believe the cost was $l7.00 for a boy's haircut and up to $40.00 for adults? We went to about five shops and finally found one that did all five for $88.00. The children know about every kids' menu in a restaurant, and we have learned a lot of ways to share meals (all legal) and get a variety of food. Nearly everyone can now read a map, which is a great help with as much as we get lost. We put close to 30,000 miles on the RV and about 3,000 of those miles are from being lost Also, we can take the bike trailer off the RV in record time when we find we are blocking traffic and can't back up because of the trailer. One of our greatest lessons has been to understand if someone needs some space GIVE IT TO THEM and immediately! Well, these are a few of the lessons we have learned, and I am sure there will be more. Isn't that part of being family?

If I get a chance I will try to send an e-mail and let you know about our Alaskan adventures. Take care and God bless you all.

Love,

Sally for all of the Worlands

CHAPTER ELEVEN

"Home at Last!"

After our sweep through the west, we got home the day before Easter, April 14, 2001. Suzannah's eighth birthday was on the 15th, and since the other three children had been able to celebrate their birthdays while we were on the road, we wanted her to have the same experience. So, on April 15, even though our house was less than 100 feet away, we all loaded back into the RV and had Suzannah's birthday party there.

Our trip to Hawaii to officially meet our 50-state objective still lay ahead of us, but we all knew the Worland family's trans-U.S.A. saga had essentially come to a close. Reflecting on our twelve months on America's highways and byways, I realized that I had learned as much as the children, although most of my education was experiential while theirs was a blend of experience and homeschool academics. One of my strongest impressions was of the incredible beauty that we found in every one of the fifty states, along with the wonderful diversity they offered geographically, culturally, and socially.

Although I had been to all fifty states before we set off across the country as a family, some of my earlier opinions changed as we took an extended look at each state. For instance, my initial thoughts about California had not been the most positive. Before I got married, I had visited southern California and had departed very unimpressed — too crowded, too busy, and too liberal for my way of thinking. But after seeing the wonders of Yosemite National Park and other parts of northern California, I realized this state itself offers a wondrous variety and a beauty that few states can rival.

Isn't it good to mature in our thinking and to have our long-established opinions challenged from time to time, just to see if they still hold true? Along our trip, the children had recognized how David and I were maturing, but in a different way. They were quick to point out how the quantity of gray hair on our heads seemed to multiply as our journey continued. Well, at least I'm grateful that Proverbs 20:29 says "gray hair (is) the splendor of the old."

Planning to Return to "Real Life"

One thing we talked about after our trip was over and we came back home was how to re-engage our life, getting back in the day-to-day routines of school, church, and home, without truly getting back into the same routine we were in before. As David said in an earlier chapter, during our time away we experienced the sweetness of being able to devote attention, focus, and effort toward one another — something that seems lost in our society today. We talked with the kids about how we are just too fast-paced in our lives, holding high expectations for different activities and setting goals for getting involved in so many (too many) things.

Today, our culture defines success or importance not so much by the depth of understanding we have of each other, the wisdom we can gain as individuals, or the commitment to dedicate the time and access needed to really be able to learn from each other. Instead, society tends to characterize success by our busyness, going in many directions seemingly all at the same time, and seeing how many different things we do.

Some people might view this as experiencing life to the fullest, but in reality, when we move so fast and do so much, we can tend to become somewhat shallow. As the Worland family returned to Hidden Hollow, in Chickamauga, Georgia our desire was to define our family boundaries much more narrowly so we could continue going much deeper with one another relationally and experientially.

Much of contemporary life today, at least in our country, is complicated, but our determination has been to reduce the complications whenever possible. We yearn for our family to enjoy and somehow maintain a simple life, uncluttered by external demands and expectations, but we're realistic enough to know that with four children, even if each is involved in only one activity, we just can't avoid some degree of complexity. But, at least we would prefer to pick and choose our own complications, rather than to "become so well-adjusted to your culture that you fit into it without even thinking," as Eugene H. Petersen paraphrases Romans 12:2 in *The Message.*

Bidding Our Home on Wheels Farewell

The Coachman Leprechaun, which had served as "home" for the Worlands from mid-2000 to May of 2001, became history for us in January of 2002. We had been warned that because we had customized the RV, with the two sets of bunk beds for the children, we probably would have a difficult time finding a buyer, but we were able to sell it fairly quickly. And amazingly, the woman who bought it — a grandmother — said the reason she liked it was specifically because of the bunk beds. They would be perfect for her grandchildren, she said, for times when she would "borrow" them from their parents and take them on vacation.

Saying good-bye to it was sad for the kids, and we all miss it. We had became attached to it, and had built many memories in it as we traveled from state to state. But even that has been a valuable lesson: as life progresses, there are people and things that are with us for only a season, then we must leave them behind. The much-loved RV served as a good example of that for the children.

Bonuses

A few weeks after we had concluded our trip, David and I put pen to paper to compare the overall cost of our trip with what it would have cost the Foundation if they had elected to send him alone on the trips to the more than forty cities we visited.

Basically, we determined the expense was about break-even. Actually, we may have saved the Foundation a bit of money and at the same time, the experiences we had together as a family were priceless. We never could have afforded the trip ourselves — the RV alone would have been a tremendous stretch for us financially — so it had been an incredible opportunity, made possible in a way we could never have imagined. You couldn't have asked for a more win-win situation than that.

Being a person who has always enjoyed the adventure of doing new things, it was rewarding for me to be able to impart the same spirit to our children, helping them to realize that life in itself is an adventure, whether traversing a great country or just carrying out our daily routine.

While we cooked out a lot at the many campgrounds where we stayed, we also became virtual food critics at restaurants from coast to coast. The kids became intimately acquainted with the kids' menus at both sit-down and fast-food eateries, and we all learned about sharing meals (in keeping with restaurant policies) so everyone could experience a variety of food.

By the time we were halfway through the trip, most of us had become experts at reading maps, too, which was a great help at times when we got lost. Actually, we estimate that of the more than 30,000 miles we logged in the RV, about 3,000 of those could be attributed to times when we did lose our way, wound up going in a wrong direction, and then had to backtrack.

And if you ever need a bicycle trailer removed in record time from behind your RV, particularly if you find yourself blocking traffic and can't back up because of the trailer, we're the folks to call. We are, as they say, very experienced in that!

Interestingly, throughout our trip we experienced virtually no poor health, even though we frequently encountered dramatic changes in weather. We all had a cold or two, but nothing more serious than that. After we returned home, however, it seemed like disease bacteria were trying to make up for lost time. Perhaps it's because our immunities had gotten low while we were away, relatively sheltered from people outside of our family in the cloistered environment of the RV. I'm not sure, but after the kids got back into school, it seemed as if they caught every virus that was going around. The Worland kids, who prior to the trip had earned perfect attendance awards at school for years, each were having to take absences due to an assortment of illnesses.

One week after the children had returned to school in the fall, we had what I called "the battle of the temperatures." One child had a fever of 102.2 degrees, another had a temperature of 103.1, and then Bonny Jean won the "prize" for the highest fever: 104.1. That was our worst single week after returning home, but for a while it seemed that the kids were engaged in a germ-collecting competition. Thinking back to how we had prayed for good health on the trip, I don't think we fully appreciated how vitally important that was.

Some Surprises for Our Return

It would be nice to say that after our trip across America concluded, we quickly were able to resume normal activities. Craig and Scott, for instance, were eager to get back to organized basketball. However, despite all we had done to give the boys an opportunity to practice their basketball skills on their own, two weeks before the tryouts for the eighth grade team, Craig hurt his knee badly. Before we left, the coach had indicated the time away would not be detrimental to Craig's making the team the following year, but it didn't work out that way. He received the devestating news that he did not make the team.

When he found out he hadn't made the team, Craig was crushed, feeling as if his whole world had been taken away from him. Initially, he blamed it largely on being away for a year. "It's because of that stupid trip that I didn't get on the basketball team!" he said, but to his credit, Craig never repeated that statement. We talked about the reality in life that things don't always go as planned, and even at his young age, he realized that the trip offered him a lot more that what he could have gained from playing one season of basketball. This helped to mediate some of his hurt, and he became more determined to play next year. He said that "he would work so hard the coach would be sorry he didn't put him on the team." And work hard he did!

On a more positive note, the long-awaited pets that our children wanted were quickly added to our family once our travels had ceased. The children had understood why, as much as a year before our trip started, they could not add any pets because we didn't want to be concerned with their care while we were gone. But once we settled in back home, the kids were insistent in their desire to start filling that void.

By one week after our return from Hawaii, the children had all gone to select their new pets, with the boys each choosing a dog and the girls each settling on a kitten. All four of the new animals, we reminded them, were to remain of the outdoor variety. That was one small way to retain a measure of simplicity by not having to train and clean up after indoor pets. We also added one horse to the three we had boarded in our absence.

Mission Accomplished – What's Next?

David's work with the National Christian Foundation continues to be rewarding. Today he is helping to facilitate strategic foundations that have affiliated with NCF, providing office administration services as well as meeting with donors, local ministries, and professional advisors. As David says, "We'll do whatever is needed to help them in equipping and training the leadership of their organizations, providing answers to specific questions, and helping to resolve key issues that many of them encounter as they reach out to their communities in the name of Christ."

He also is involved with the Association of Christian Community Foundations. Its role is to help local foundations evaluate what they could accomplish by networking together compared to what they have been able to do independently. Again, he finds it gratifying to see how the principles of "Two are better than one, because they have a good return for their work.... A cord of three strands is not quickly broken" (Ecclesiastes 4:9-12), and "As iron sharpens iron, so one man sharpens another" (Proverbs 27:17) apply so naturally to charitable foundations.

What a Difference a Year Makes

We each returned from our trip as different people. The children, of course, were all one year older and more mature, I believe in every possible way. One thing I noticed as we were traveling — and this remained true after we had settled into home living again — was that they had become more adventuresome, more confident to go into new situations, or to interact with people they didn't know.

Scott already has told us that after he graduates from college, he wants to continue building upon his traveling experiences. He would like to live in a number of different countries for several months at a time so he can learn things about each nation: its people, its language, and its culture.

When we returned from the trip, one of our priorities was to find a church with a very good, strong youth group. As the kids get older, this becomes a greater need for them, both spiritually and socially. In the midst of our search for such a program, we found the newfound confidence our children had gained also had some drawbacks, since they suddenly felt they were ready to make decisions for our family — decisions we needed to make together, not independently.

For instance, the boys enjoyed a summer retreat at one church in particular and concluded on their own that should become "our" church. Unfortunately, it is about a forty-five-minute drive from our home and to have to make that trip several times a week, in addition to all the traveling we already do for school and extracurricular activities, would add another layer of stress that we didn't need. After seeing the benefits of a simplified, less cluttered lifestyle during our trip, our desire was to simplify our lives. We didn't know if we agreed with their church plan, even though it offered many appealing programs and activities.

Then we found a church only about ten minutes from our home with a large, very well-planned youth and music program. Bonny Jean and Suzannah loved it. The boys, however, seemed determined not to cooperate, failing to understand why becoming regularly involved in a church forty-five minutes away was such a problem. So, the process continued.

A Journey Starts with a Single Step

One morning not long ago, I looked outside and became enraptured by perhaps the most glorious sunrise I had ever seen. It was beautiful, with vivid oranges and pinks filling the clouds. As I turned toward the west, however, I saw nothing but dark gray clouds that were slowly being dispelled by the brilliance of the rising sun. I thought what a wonderful metaphor those contrasting views were for the adventure my family had just concluded.

As individuals, we need to be willing to step out and do something unique. In our case, it was to literally set foot in each of the fifty states. Our dream turned out to be unbelievable, even greater than we ever could have hoped. But this beautiful experience started out very slowly, much like the sunrise that captivated me that morning. In fact, before the trip became a reality, there were times when our optimistic dream was clouded by doubts, wondering how God could ever bring it about.

Recently, a friend made a major career change. After years of diligently serving the nonprofit organization that employed him, he reached the point when it seemed that he had "been there, done that" and felt an urging to strike out and do something very different. Sometimes using the analogy that he felt somewhat like a thoroughbred race horse that had become stuck pulling a plow, he determined that what he really wanted to do was to be freed up to do what God had uniquely equipped him to do. Just as we didn't know what would make our U.S.A. trip happen, my friend didn't know how the Lord would bring about his change in vocation. In fact, he wasn't even certain what that change would look like specifically, but when the opportunity finally presented itself, he was ready and stepped out in faith. Today, he says he feels more fulfilled in his work than he has for many years.

Do you see how this analogy can fit your life? It might just be a very special activity, or a major life change, but as we begin to let God use our lives and simply follow His leading, we will find Him transforming our lives into something more and more beautiful. Best of all, we can be a witness to others of how the Lord can use us in different ways, ways that often run counter to the pattern established by the world around us. As our son said, "Why can't we just be a *normal* family?"

Yes, there is a risk. Even as followers of Christ, sometimes we feel afraid to present too much of a contrast to our culture. We feel more comfortable blending in, being just like the rest of the gray clouds around us, but if we're willing to step out, little by little we will become the human equivalent of those brilliant orange and pink and red clouds that signal the dawning of a promising new day. It will become more evident to everyone that we are doing what Jesus Christ wants us to do — and what a light to the world we will be!

Awsome Opportunities within Our Grasp

September 11, 2001, made a profound difference in our national psyche. The buoyant optimism most of us shared prior to that tragic day was dispelled. In its place, feelings of anxiety, uncertainty, and restlessness have increased dramatically. But our family's odyssey showed us that even amid the tragedy, pain, and heartache that we experience in everyday life, not to mention the unplanned happenings like terrorist attacks, there remained an incredible opportunity for each of us to do something marvelous, to live our lives to the fullest.

For you and your family, this may not mean acquiring an RV and crisscrossing the United States. It may be something very different. But whatever that special undertaking would be you need to be willing to reach outside of the "box" that makes up your normal, comfortable existence and do something very different, something so far beyond your particular norm that you will never be the same after you have done it.

Those of us who are followers of Jesus Christ, in particular, are called to transcend the hum-drum of every day and, as David says, engage as ordinary people in extraordinary pursuits for the glory of God and His kingdom. It could be taking an extended missions trip, maybe even as an entire family. It could be exploring a very special area of interest, something that has long held great appeal for you, but until this point you have not taken the initiative to commit yourself to it. It could be engaging in some very meaningful, even life-changing endeavor in your community, something that becomes "a major focal" point of your life for some length of time.

The key, I believe, is recognizing that even though we all are just ordinary people, each of us can still participate in something extraordinary. One recent morning, as I was involved in another morning of getting each of the kids ready for school, I was reflecting on just how normal we really are: each of the children moving at their own pace, typical conflict among siblings with decidedly different personalities, and sometimes struggles with the stress of school assignments and imminent exams.

There are many times when we, the adults, as well as the kids, do things that certainly are not God-like. Yes, we are as normal as any family I know. But by recognizing our failures we are reminded of how far we are from being what we really want our family to be, as well as being the kind of people God wants us to be.

Reminder of How Things Can Be

During these hectic moments, it's fun now to think back on how nice it was while we were on the trip and able to devote so much time just to one another as a family, without the inevitable rushing here and there that we once again do so often. When the children are being uncooperative or unpleasant to one another, I'll always remember how pleasant things were — and how they can be again, if we just take the effort to step off our daily treadmill, at least for a little while. I don't know if we will ever again be able to do something as elaborate as our U.S.A. trip, but I value how it enhanced our relationships as a family, as well as how it strengthened each of us individually. I suppose that's why I have been urging other people to take on something like it for their own family, even if it doesn't require 30,000 miles in an RV and many more miles in airplanes.

Our family will never be the same, and if you're willing to venture outside the "box" and do something especially creative and unusual, you'll never be the same either. "Why can't we just be a normal family" certainly has a new meaning to us.

We go through much of each day forgetting to honor God. For those of us who sincerely trust in Jesus Christ, this is not intentional. We just get so busy with demands and activities that we temporarily "forget" to keep the Lord first. The fact is He is nearer than a heartbeat. That is one reason I would strongly urge you to consider: what will push you out of your comfortable, familiar "box" and into an unusual, life-changing experience for you and your loved ones, and perhaps even change and enhance your relationships, and pushing you into a relationship or changing your relationship with the living God?

The beginning of the Westminster Catechism states that "the chief end of man is to glorify God and enjoy Him forever." Certainly, we can do that as we go through a typical day: working, cooking, cleaning, carpooling, visiting with friends, talking on the phone, catching up with the news. But if we are willing to step outside the routine, to undertake something very different that will stretch us and challenge us, our understanding of what it really means to glorify God and enjoy Him forever will take on a new significance.

Home at Last

Birthdays in the RV

The kids were so happy to walk down our 1/2 mile driveway

Left to Right:
Scott, Suzannah, Bonny Jean, and Craig

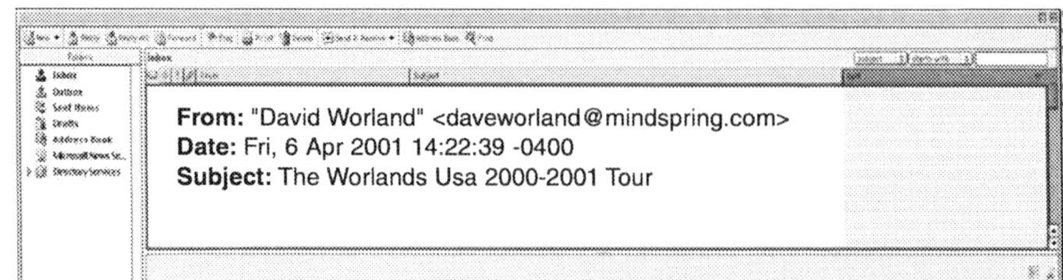
From: "David Worland" <daveworland@mindspring.com>
Date: Fri, 6 Apr 2001 14:22:39 -0400
Subject: The Worlands Usa 2000-2001 Tour

Dear Family and Friends,

Hello from Girdwood, Alaska. We are in a beautiful place with the snow-capped mountains all around us. We are at the Alyeska Resort, where we are all staying in one room called the Jr. Suite. I believe we have pushed the kids' tolerance level pretty far and they look forward to home where they can have their space. The resort is about 45 minutes south of Anchorage in the Chugach Mountains.

We were not being successful in finding dog sledding as most companies had closed for the season. We were so happy when we discovered that there was a group still operating near the resort. We had a wonderful time riding through the woods and over the fields through beautiful snow, and looking up at the mountains as we rode in the sled. The children all got to mush the dogs, which was really neat.

"Ignorance is bliss" sure has new meaning to me. Some of you may say " You can't teach an old dog new tricks." We went skiing, which I had done a few times many years ago but I had never taken a lesson. I had gotten where I could go down pretty moderate trails. Well, David and I both took a lesson, and I realized I had to relearn almost everything. I basically stayed on the same slope all day trying to master the basics. I watched our four children, who we had made sure had lessons from the get-go, doing wonderfully as they progressed from one slope to another. They also took snowboarding lessons, which the boys decided was their favorite. It was really neat to see the next generation doing so well after having the advantage of lessons at the beginning. If your children are really interested in learning any new sport or hobby I recommend good coaching and teaching at the beginning. It sure is easier to learn correctly than to learn all over. You also need to help them learn "when to come out of the cold." Suzannah complained of her feet being cold; when I took her inside and discovered she had come out of her snow boots while building a snowman and her feet were soaking wet. I took off the wet socks, and one foot was really very cold. It really concerned me for frost bite, and she was in tears as I tried to warm it. I finally got it warm, and I asked her why she had not said anything earlier. She said, "I was having so much fun I didn't want to stop playing."

We had snow and clouds every day until yesterday when we had planned a plane ride over the glaciers. Yesterday was beautiful, and we had a magnificent plane ride and saw gorgeous blue ice glaciers, with crevices at least 1000 feet deep, the Prince William Sound, the Turnagan arm, Lake George, Fjords (where the glaciers meet the Pacific ocean), glaciers calving (breaking away), and buffalo. It was spectacular. We then drove about 150 miles to Talkeetna, where you have the best view of Mount McKinley. As we were driving the clouds returned and we asked Bonny Jean to pray that they might move so that we could see the mountain. Well, she prayed that the mountain would move. I guess that is the faith of the mustard seed. Thankfully, God decided to leave the mountain but move the clouds, and we had a spectacular view of the awesome Mount McKinley. While we were looking at the mountain, two young men walked up and we had a wonderful visit. Sasha had climbed almost to the top and wanted to try again, and Mark was preparing to climb the mountain next to McKinley, which is called Mt. Hunter. We had prayer together and felt inspired after being with them. Craig and Scott sure listened intently to these two guys who had done so many exciting things, and I could see our boys were planning their own adventures. When we left we reminded them they could always do neat adventures without having to move so far away! This trip sure has given them all wings to want to do more exploring.

It has been wonderful to have this vacation time as David has had a chance to relax. Sometimes, at home, it is hard for him to separate work from vacation. This has been great.

We fly out at about 1:00 AM (Sat. morning) and then we drive to Spokane, Washington, where David has a meeting with someone interested in setting up a foundation. He is meeting with them Saturday afternoon. I hope he can stay awake for the meeting after the late flight and driving time. It seems his work energizes him.

We will begin our trip home finishing up the last three states in the "lower 48." While we are all looking forward to being home it is with a twinge of regret our long-planned-for-trip will soon be complete.
We do look forward to seeing everyone and hope you are all well.

Take care and stay in touch.

Love, Sally, David, Craig, Scott, Bonny Jean, and Suzannah

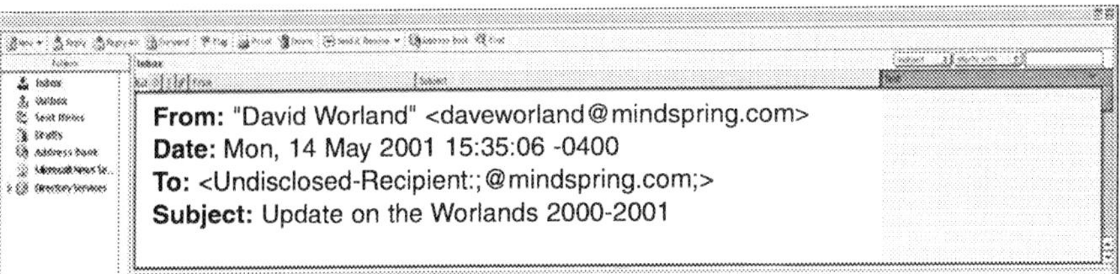

From: "David Worland" <daveworland@mindspring.com>
Date: Mon, 14 May 2001 15:35:06 -0400
To: <Undisclosed-Recipient:;@mindspring.com;>
Subject: Update on the Worlands 2000-2001

May 14, 2001

Dear Family and Friends,

Aloha from Hawaii. Well, we are now in the 50th state of the Union as well as our 50th state. As we got off the airplane in Honolulu, we all gave each other the "high five." What a neat feeling we have knowing we have been to all fifty states together. About Twenty-three years ago I began to save my frequent flyer points from Delta so that one day I could take my "hoped for family" on a trip such as this. Of course, I wasn't even married at that time and was enjoying my single life, so I guess you can say I was a planner and a dreamer. David had quite a few frequent flyer points so we were able to combine them and had enough points to fly the family for free.

As we arrived in Honolulu on the evening of May 10th, we were told it would be easy to find our hotel just a few minutes away. Well, we drove for about an hour and finally stopped a policeman who tried to give us directions after using his cell phone several times to call the hotel. Finally he said, "just let me take you there." So here we were our first night in Hawaii with a police escort. I guess the police would make up for the park rangers we kept so busy on the mainland. Well, we drove around following him and stopping every so often for him to use his cell phone. He took us to a hotel that was not the correct one so we motioned to him again and once again the "cell phone and following " began. Finally, he stops and shares with us he discovered that hotel had changed names, and we had driven past it several times. So, we finally reached our destination of our hotel at about midnight. I felt I was sleep-walking from our six-hour time change. When we checked in, they had given away our adjoining rooms. As I stood at the hotel front desk trying to decide my reaction something "better than me" intervened, and I remained calm. Anyway the desk clerk said "let me check on something." He came back and said, "I am going to give you a fat room (which he explained means really nice) for the same price." Well, we came up to one of the top floors and discovered we were in a two-bedroom suite with windows all around the front and side giving us a view of the city and the ocean from the rooms and balcony. The room would have been $545.00 a night, but he gave it to us for the same price as the ajoining rooms would have been. The suite has a kitchen so we have been able to buy groceries to help with the very expensive food cost. What a FAT room!

We have really toured the Island and have been to the pineapple fields, Diamond Head Crater, Paradise Cove for a luau, visiting with cousins, have had the famous shaved ice twice, tried hula dancing, saw fire dancing, shopping, swam in the ocean at the Banzai pipeline, and today we go snorkeling and tomorrow to the big Island on a small plane where we will spend the day touring, and even see the volcanoes.

As we head home and back into our daily living, I hope things will never seem routine and that we will be able to reflect on all we have learned as a family from this wonderful experience. We are appreciative to NCF and all of you who have supported us in doing something "different." I am thankful to my husband David for always being willing to do something unique and show his support to his family through his love and his attempts to be there for each of us. I have learned so much about my children through homeschooling them and spending 24 - 7 with them. David and I celebrated our 17th anniversary while in Hawaii, and we both agreed that then while it might have been "romantic" to come by ourselves we are very thankful for the four precious children we were able to bring with us. They are truly on "loan to us from God," and we hope we will be better parents through the things we have learned from the experience of this year's travel. We know God ordained this trip, and that " with God all things are possible" and to Him may we give the praise and the glory and to remember "the chief end of man is to glorify God and enjoy Him forever."

With Love,

Sally, David, Craig, Scott, Bonny Jean, and Suzannah

CHAPTER TWELVE

Treasuring and Training Our Kids

I believe that it is so important to let kids be kids. With four children in our family, having each one involved in just one activity means David and I do a lot of running back and forth, taking them wherever they need to go. I know there are some parents who would resent this, but I see it as time that we are investing in our kids. In fact, often we drive to the school and pick up three children but leave one behind to participate in whatever sport practice or activity that is happening that day. We bring the other children home so they can enjoy being at the house, playing on our property, or just getting some time to do what they want to do. Then I make the return trip to pick up the other child. Certainly there are days when it would be a lot easier for all of us to stay at the school and wait until the other one is finished, but that would take away from the time the other kids can spend at home.

It's important to us for them to be able to spend a lot of time at home just to get outside and ride their horses, explore the creeks, the woods, and the other natural wonders God has provided. As I said before, I believe from the bottom of my heart that kids need the chance just to be kids. It bothers me to hear an adult say a child is not mature. They are not supposed to be mature, they are children!

I thought about this one day when the girls were in the living room making Valentine's cards for friends at school, and the boys were outside playing basketball. Whether indoors or outdoors, we have intentionally tried to give the children plenty of time to be themselves, to play and enjoy being kids. There will be ample time later for them to be-and to act like-adults.

At times, children need structure, there's no question about that. But so many kids these days are too structured, with sports, piano lessons, girls' choir, boys' choir, Scouts, and all kinds of other things, that they don't have time for themselves. A philosophy David and I have adopted is that if there is something the kids want to do that they can only do as a child, such as Boy Scouts or Girl Scouts, or youth choir, or playing youth sports, we encourage them to do it. Things they can do as adults can wait.

A Growing Experience for All

As we embarked on our trip, we knew that Craig and Scott were entering adolescence, a time of transition that many parents dread. I think being with them so constantly on the trip helped us to ease them through that stage and all of the emotions that come with it. We talk with the boys on more of an adult level now, and they feel free to share their views with us on subjects that we probably wouldn't have discussed before the U.S.A. trip.

Frankly, over the years that I had envisioned making this trip with my family, I didn't anticipate that a deepened intimacy among all six of us would prove to be one of the foremost benefits. I had expected the fun, the excitement of discovery, and the challenges of "following some kind of schedule." But simply being together, day after day, week after week, without competition from friends, family, school, church, and other activities, proved far more meaningful than I could have imagined. We came back with sixty rolls of film, discs of digital photos, and six or seven videotapes, but the most valuable "souvenirs" we brought home were the deepened relationships we built over the miles and the heightened sense of appreciation we developed for one another.

As we were returning home I began to realize how much I missed many things about where we live some majestic and some simple. How good to come home to the beautiful mountains, pastures, lakes, and wildlife. It was so good to be back to the quaint churches, corner country markets, and something we call our "country mall." It is called the Flintstone Farm and Garden and has everything needed for farming, pet care, and even overalls. It has expanded its buildings and now also houses an auto repair shop, a dog obedience traning school, and a knife and sword shop. There is also Janice's Hairshop where we can get a haircut as well as the most practical advice to any problem we may have. And it is certainly at a much better price than therapy! After shopping and getting our hair done we can eat at Karens Restaurant, "with Mary's home cooking." What more could we want?

About one week after we had returned home, Suzannah and Bonny Jean treated me to a "Happy-I-Love-You Day," complete with breakfast in bed. That meant so much to me, and I think to the girls as well, but what we learned about each other on the trip made this occasion extra special.

Emphasizing What's Most Important

For both David and me, our faith in Jesus Christ is the most important thing in our lives. We are thankful that each of our children have made the commitment to follow Christ. It is our prayer that they might know when it seems everything else "fails" He is truly enough. For this reason, one family activity we have observed for years is putting Bible verses on the refrigerator, and before an agreed upon date, the children have to be able to recite the verse before they eat dinner. We usually give them several days to learn the assigned verse, not only so they can commit it to memory, but also so they can begin discovering how to apply it to their hearts and minds. It's become kind of a joke in our family that the verses have to come out before the food can go in.

One day, Craig (then an eighth grader) commented that although they are required to learn many Bible verses as part of the curriculum at their Christian school, the verses he remembers the most are the ones I taught the children when they were little, reviewing them over and over again. There would be times when we'd be hiking somewhere on our property and I would shout, "Give me a verse!" and one of the children would begin reciting a verse we had learned, and another child would finish it.

Obviously, we make allowances for the differences in ages as they learned the verses. For Suzannah, the learning process has been a little slower, partly because after she joined our family, just learning the English language, and all that is involved in that was challenge enough. So for her, sometimes we have selected simpler verses, but in any case the principle is the same: learning to hide God's Word in our hearts, as we are urged to do in Psalm 119:11.

One of our favorites, which tied very closely to our trip around the United States, is Ecclesiates 4:9, 10, which says, "Two are better than one, because they have a good return for their work; if one falls down, his friend can help him up...." There have been many times that we have appreciated having one another around to assist when we stumbled in one way or another!

Managing Conflict

There are times when an incident in our family prompts the selection of a particular verse. For instance, if an argument occurs between two or more of the children, it seems appropriate for them to learn what God says about being kind and loving to one another. We definitely are a normal family, with at least the usual assortment of imperfections, so it's helpful to look at what the Lord tells us through His Word to give us a standard for what our thoughts and actions should be.

Another way we resolve conflict in our home is by implementing a very practical way of encouraging our children to cool off. Once we enter the driveway into our property, it is about half a mile to our house, so sometimes when one of the children has been argumentative or unkind to another sibling after school, I will simply stop the car and invite him or her to get out and run home. Hopefully, by the time they get home, they have used up at least some of their excess energy in a productive way so they can be a little more kind to one another.

Not long ago, Bonny Jean had been rude to Suzannah on the way home from school, so after we had talked about her behavior at length, as we turned into the driveway, she volunteered, "I want to get out of the car and walk." I stopped the car and told her that when she got to the house, I wanted her to sit down and write a note to Suzannah, listing five positive things about her sister to make up for her rudeness.

Bonny Jean did better than that. She stopped along the way, took out a piece of paper and a pencil from her school bag, sat down, and wrote the note before she got home. When she arrived at the house, Bonny Jean not only had written the five positive observations about Suzannah, but also her attitude was greatly improved.

Since Craig and Scott are only thirteen months apart in age, they have always been very close as friends and very supportive of one another in sports and other activities. They also have conflicts, however, and sometimes get angry enough to wrestle and fight, even though that doesn't happen very often. We have made rules against physical and verbal assault in our family, and the children abide by them fairly well. When the boys do have differences, they typically get over them very quickly, while the girls generally don't resolve their conflict as easily. So the "cooling off" trek from the top of the driveway to the house can be a great healer for them.

Closing Thoughts

The reason we love the area where we live so much, in addition to its natural beauty, is the opportunity it has provided our children to be outside and be creative, to learn to make their own fun—an ability that it seems is being lost among many children today, particularly in the U.S.A. We are not opposed to TV or computers or video games, but we always try to stress that kids don't have to be inside watching TV to be kept busy, or so busy that they don't have time to be spontaneous and just have fun doing something new. Sports are good for children, teaching much-needed discipline, cooperation, and commitment, but we have purposefully tried to limit structured time in such a way that it leaves plenty of freedom to play and just have fun, without any other purpose in mind. We also realize if they play high school sports, cheerleading, band, etc., it will require a great time commitment. So, for now we want them to enjoy the freedom to play as kids.

I have always felt that home should be a haven, a safe place for children—where they can be themselves and receive the acceptance and affection that they need so much. A concern that I have is that a lot of parents seem to want their children to grow up so fast.

Where schooling is concerned we take one year and one child at a time. As each child is unique so should be their schooling choices. I have found positives in public, private, and Christian schools. I thoughly enjoy homeschooling and will continue to homeschool one or all if I feel it is best for them. There are years when I have felt one child needed to be homeschooled, and indeed it has been a wonderful bonding time as well as a time for them to learn how to become more independent studiers. It gives them security to feel that I am concerned about their needs.

Traditions are very important in our family and help us all to have that good sense of belonging. We have found traditions don't need to be elaborate and orchestrated, just unique to our family.

As I close I would like to share the deep sense of gratitude we have for being able to make this trip. We appreciate the National Christian Foundation for allowing David to work in this manner, making it possible for us to engage in such a unique adventure, as well as family and friends who also supported us in doing "something different." "Why can't we just be a normal family" has more meaning than it ever has. God desires that we live life to the fullest, experiencing His goodness, grace and mercies forever.

There are always pressures that pull against the family, including good activities with friends. While we appreciate the times our children can spend with their friends, we always have stressed the need for us to do things just as a family. At times this even means saying "no" to the children when they are asked to do something else because we have already made plans as a family.

Occasionally, the kids will complain, but in most cases they understand the importance of our spending time together as a family. And as a result of being together for so much time on our U.S.A. trip, we gained a greater appreciation of one another and enjoy being with one another more than ever.

One day, I believe, the children will be especially appreciative of our insistence that we spend time as a family. We point out that friends will come and go, but our family will always be the same. These times we spend together are truly once-in-a-lifetime. One day the children all will be independent and have their own families, but the times we insisted on being together will be invaluable memories.

We have a very affectionate family-We feel it's so important that, when opportunities present themselves, we show affection to one another. This may mean a hug, or something as simple as David or I stroking one of our children's shoulders while we are sitting in church. In fact, in church we have them captive and can enjoy that time on the pew with them! We want them to have the security of knowing we are always there for them, and that we love them. We find that even as our older children are moving into their teenage years, they still need affection-even if they don't want to admit it or act as if they need it.

The time on this earth goes by so quickly. Whether you are single or married may I encourage you to "live outside the box." Venture into the unknown and know that God is truly your closest friend. Through Christ we have the ultimate freedom, the freedom to be what we imagine, desire, and dream. Each month, day, or hour can be a new beginning for those not willing to be "just normal."

During our stay in Hawaii, David and I celebrated our Seventeenth wedding anniversary. While we agreed it might have been romantic for us to be there alone, we were so thankful for the four precious children we were able to bring with us. Knowing they truly are on loan to us from God, we trust that through this experience we have grown to become better parents and that as a whole, we have bonded together more closely as a family.

There is no question in my mind that the Lord ordained this trip, even from the time He planted the seed of the idea in my mind, finally bringing it into fruition more than two decades later. What better evidence, we thought, of the reality that, as the theme verse for our trip declares, "with God all things are possible" (Luke 1:37).